The
STRENGTH OF SAINTS

Also by A. LaFaye:

The
STRENGTH OF SAINTS

A. LAFAYE

Simon & Schuster Books for Young Readers
New York   London   Toronto   Sydney   Singapore

SIMON & SCHUSTER BOOKS FOR YOUNG READERS
An imprint of Simon & Schuster Children's Publishing Division
1230 Avenue of the Americas, New York, New York 10020

Book design by O'Lanso Gabbidon
The text for this book is set in Garamond.
Printed in the United States of America
2 4 6 8 10 9 7 5 3 1
Library of Congress Cataloging-in-Publication Data
LaFaye, A.
The Strength of Saints / by A. LaFaye.
p. cm.
Sequel to: Nissa's place.
Summary: In 1936, fourteen-year-old Nissa takes a stand against racial prejudice and for her own integrity and independence, drawing on the support of her individualistic mother, her father, stepmother, and some of the inhabitants of their Louisiana town.
ISBN 0-689-83200-1
[1. Conduct of life—Fiction. 2. Race relations—Fiction. 3. Mothers and daughters—Fiction. 4. Remarriage—Fiction. 5. City and town life—Louisiana—Fiction. 6. Louisiana—Fiction] I. Title.
PZ7.L1413 Su 2002
[Fic]—dc21
2001032072

FIRST
EDITION

To Sarah,
the librarian who always
strives to do the right thing

Once again David Gale has helped me take a literary peek into the lives of the folks of Harper. Thanks, David. I'd also like to thank Stephanie Owens Lurie for demanding to know what happens next. I hope you enjoy the results, Stephanie. Thanks to Elena Murphy for her help in the editing process. I'd also like to thank all the copyeditors, designers, publicists, booksellers, bookstores, parents, teachers, and kids who have supported the Nissa books so far. Most importantly thank you God for the inspiration to write this book—it traveled through me like the wind.

Contents

Worry Walking

*P*apa was in trouble. Not in a devil's-going-to-chase-him-down sort of way. Truth be told, I wasn't right certain what pulled Papa out of bed to pace the upstairs hallway. Any number of things could've been the culprit. In the spring of '36, he had a new baby daughter under our roof—young Miss Lily Maeve, with her sausage link toes—he might've been worrying after her welfare. My baby brother, Benjamin, died as an itty-bitty thing. Born sickly, he never did grow into his health. The thought that Lily might fall sick haunted him. The idea of it settled into Papa's heart when his new wife, Lara, went into labor near about a month early. On the day of Lily's birth Dr. Swenson had to swear on his soul to get Papa to believe that the baby would be just fine. That promise still didn't strangle Papa's fears. They cropped back up like nasty old weeds anytime Lily so much as sneezed.

Papa got so frenzied, Dr. Swenson took to stopping by our place on his way to the office he keeps in the train station. Lara had a cup of tea with lemon and pepper sitting on the porch post each morning. Papa'd bring Lily Maeve out and act like he just wanted to say how do. Dr. Swenson would scoop that baby girl up. In making a show of tickling her and teasing her, he'd give her a right quick examination. Those morning visits kept Papa sane.

Papa didn't forget about me amongst all his worrying over Lily Maeve. No, he fretted over me, too. My health had him concerned as well, but not in the same fashion. I hadn't so much as had a cold for as long as we could both remember. The trouble with me was that I ran the town libraries. Not such a dangerous thing on the face of it, but since I checked books out to colored folks and white folks alike in a town like Harper, Louisiana, I took as many risks as a fool who decided to build a house on the Carolina coastline in the middle of hurricane season.

Knowing the folks in Tucumsett Parish had a reputation for taking a match to places where the color line wasn't carefully observed, I'd divided Lara's old house right down the middle, making the libraries of Harper—both East and West. Invoking the old separate-but-equal law—heavy on the equal—appeased most folks, but there were a whole mess of fools in town who figured they had a right to ask who'd been reading the books they checked out.

Why, one day, Mrs. Linzy, our pastor's wife, brought some silly old novel up to me and asked, "Is this here book clean, Nissa?"

Figuring she had her mind on sneezing, I said, "I can't keep this one on the shelves long enough for it to collect dust, Mrs. Linzy."

"I'm not talking about dust, child." She darted her eyes over to the door that leads to the West Harper Library.

Knowing Mrs. Linzy didn't get her idea of unclean things out of any Bible, I said, "Why, this here book is as clean as a newly baptized baby."

In fact it'd been in close proximity to such a child. Mrs. Villeneuve, who can trace her ancestry straight to Crispus Atticus, had the book in her lap when they christened Otis Dupree's little niece Avida at Revival Baptist the Sunday before last.

Of course I didn't tell mean old Mrs. Linzy any such thing. She left the library smiling and nodding, convinced her little white hands were safe.

I'd divided that library for safety's sake, but I wasn't about to keep books from folks who wanted to read them on account of the silly ideas of some soul-clouded white folks. But Papa feared I'd get caught up in my generosity one day and somebody would cinch it around my neck like a noose. This particular fear had Papa listening to every little story he heard about the libraries, as if he might be hearing reports coming back from some battlefield where his family fought for their lives.

Worrying after children is a natural part of being a papa, true enough, but that's not all that weighed on Papa's soul that spring. If prosperity were a well, then Harper's was running close to drying up. Money became more precious than water in a desert long about then. Many folks used to work in the mine across the way in Mississippi. That place had closed down near about two years earlier. Few of those folks ever found another job. The Journiettes had to cut back on their planting on account of the poor cotton prices. They didn't hire on near as many people anymore. The Minkies over at the mercantile across the street had cut off credit. They were running a cash only business. Mr. Hess, who owned the paper where Papa worked, had to cut his production in half after folks started to cancel their subscriptions. Papa had a new mouth to feed on less money once he went to working every other day.

Even that didn't stop Papa from being generous. On Saturdays, Papa helped the Minkies stock their shelves since they didn't have any family of their own and they'd started feeling their age in their joints. But they asked him to stop coming in on account of the fact they didn't have goods to spare. Mr. Minkie said it didn't seem right for such hardworking hands to go home empty. Papa helped them anyhow. That's the kind of fella Papa is—good to the pit of his soul. It's a sorry shame that goodness doesn't protect a body from worries.

Time was when Papa didn't fret over a thing. A tornado could be tearing its way through town and he'd be lounging in the downstairs hallway reading a book. But in the early weeks of April, Papa walked out his worries in the late hours with only the cicadas to keep him company.

Half a lifetime of worrying and wishing taught me neither one made life return to its old ways. A change for the better meant stepping in and remolding things. I tried to talk with Papa, help him do just that, but he turned me away.

When I joined him in the hall one night, he stood by the window overlooking the street. The leaves on the trees out front cast a shadowy web over his face. Seeing me, he said, "It's like my mind's filled with swamp gas. I can't get a single thought to travel straight these days."

I nodded.

He laughed, the kind that sounded like it might turn to tears, then added, "A baby can just gobble up the day. Night's a good time to sort things out."

"What you thinking about, Papa?" I leaned into him, resting my head against his shoulder.

Taking my hand into his, he said, "I couldn't pin a thought down to share it."

"Sounds like you need a little thinking room, Papa."

"True enough."

Kissing him on the cheek, I turned to leave, but something held me there for a bit. I don't know if it was the distant look in his eyes or the way his shoulders bent forward like they carried a sack of grain each, but it had me shivering on the inside.

If a family had a cornerstone, then Papa was just that for the Bergens. He held us all up, keeping us safe and happy. I found myself wondering, *What in God's good sense would I do if Papa fell?* I meant that in a falling-into-yourself kind of way—how a person becomes when the worries get so great, you can't even think of the world around you. Only your own thoughts exist. I got that way when my mama left.

Back in the spring of '33, she packed a suitcase and walked out the door without so much as a by your leave. I fell straight into myself and didn't come out for near to a year, worrying about whether I'd ever see my mama again, if she loved me, if our family would survive. And through all of it, Papa held me up.

When Mama calmed her roving heart and settled in Chicago, she whirled back into my life all "sorry"s and "see here"s, explaining how a body can't love another if they don't love themselves. Stepping out of my day-to-day life to spend some time with her up North, I acquired the strength to stand on my own—even returned home to build a library fit for a divided town. Papa'd talked me through every decision, letting me lead the way.

As I walked back to my room that night, I wondered if I would have the strength to hold Papa up. The sheets felt cold as I slipped into bed. Closing my eyes tight, I prayed God would guide Papa to a sense of peace so I'd never have to find out just how strong I'd become.

Lies We'd Like to Believe

Come morning, Papa wore the weight of his worry in his face, looking all drawn and pale. He carried Lily Maeve on his hip like I'd seen near about every mama do when she stood in the mercantile needing an arm to shop with. I can't say why, but it looked kind of funny to see Papa walking around with Lily hanging on his side. With his free hand, he carried a stack of books. Setting them on the table in front of me, he said, "I've read these here. You can take them to the libraries."

Smiling, I said, "No wonder you've got no time to think. You're reading your mind full up."

Papa had turned to playing with Lily's nose, so it took a minute for my words to sink in. Stubbing his toe into mine, he said, "I've got to have something to think about, now don't I, Neesay?"

Even coming in the side door didn't get Papa to tell me what troubled him. Years of knowing every little idea that sauntered through my mama's head set me to believing a child had a right to know all about a parent. Papa lived a more private life, and I still hadn't learned to keep my prying mind to myself.

"How's the Lily Maeve?" I said, rustling her hair. "How many books did Papa read to you this morning?"

"Guck!" she declared, raising her hand like she'd just answered my question clear as the water on my eye.

"She's taken a fancy to pointing out all the cats in *Millions of Cats*. She keeps trying to lick them," Papa told me as he snatched at the tip of Lily's tongue. That girl thought the world came in through her mouth—the way she stuck everything in there or licked what wouldn't fit between her lips.

"I was partial to pigs myself," I said, taking my cereal bowl to the sink.

Papa rolled his eyes. "That's a truth I'll never deny. I hunted for books with pigs until my eyes went blurry."

Giving Papa an *oink* for all his hard work, I kissed Lily, who patted my cheek in return. I said, "Well, I best be off to school. I'll see you all for dinner."

Papa gave me a peck on the cheek, saying, "Be mindful of angels and stay on course."

"Yes, sir," I called on my way to the front door.

Lara came out of the dead room as I passed. Mama called the parlor on the north side of the house the dead room. She figured folks held funerals there, said she could feel the sorrow of it in the air. We hardly ever even opened the doors to that room when Mama lived with us, but Lara had her own way of moving about the place.

"Morning, Nissa." She spoke to me, but she stared at the pile of books in my hands. "What are those for?"

"The libraries." Lara had a tendency to allow her thoughts to get tangled up with her sense. I mean, what else would I be doing walking out the door with a pile of books?

Lifting the cover of the top book, she let me know what idea blocked her reasoning. "Couldn't we sell these?"

"Don't know who could afford to buy any," I said.

"Why not send them to that fella in Baton Rouge with the bookstore?"

"That's where they came from." Apparently, Papa wasn't the only one who'd let worrying grip his mind.

Shaking her head in a way that said, "What a fool I've been," Lara said, "Of course." Looking down the hall behind me, she said, "You know, we might be able to rent out that backroom."

Following her line of sight, I said, "That'd be mighty unsettling having a stranger in our house, don't you think?" I knew how it scraped at my soul when Lara first moved in after she married Papa.

"I suppose." She sighed. "But we've got to think of something, Nissa. The prices at the mercantile are going up, and you and Lily are busting buttons."

"I know." I nodded. "We'll think of something."

Resting her hand on my shoulder, Lara said, "Don't you go worrying about it. You've got enough to tackle on your own."

"Yes, ma'am." Lara took it as her duty to see that I didn't do too much adult-type thinking before my time. She had it in her mind that I'd skipped right though my childhood on account of the fact that my mama treated me like an adult since I came into this world.

I slipped my books into the bag sitting on the coat throne by the front door. That's what I call the peculiar contraption Lara brought into our house. It's a chair with a back that climbs up the wall and ends in a mirror surrounded by coat hooks. Giving Lara's collar a tug, I said, "Here's to solutions that drop from the sky like rain."

"If only," Lara said as I stepped outside.

Heading over to my best friend Mary Carroll's two doors down, I got to thinking on the too-old too-early idea. Truth is, being half adult and half child's a right dandy way to live a life, if you know how. It means you can have a heap of fun doing a thing as silly as stomping on a watermelon. Or you can work your way through something as awful as losing your mama without forfeiting your soul in the bargain.

"Morning, Nissa." Mary came down her front steps one at a time. I still missed how she used to just jump from landing to street, but Mary had gone the route of womanhood of late—never wore britches, always had her hair in ribbons and curls. Turning fifteen had killed the tomboy I used to know—a fact that made me want to spit every time I thought on it. I prayed I'd never allow myself to fade into the feminine. Seemed like turning a traitor on yourself. Being a year younger meant I had some time to prepare myself against such things.

"Morning, Mary."

Like two cows moseying to the barn for milking, we turned right toward Quince Road to head to school. We'd been walking that way for years now. Mary's brothers Teddy and Anthony headed out before us, so we didn't have to deal with their sassy nonsense. We could just amble on and talk sensible.

"Can you imagine being an uncle when you're three?" Mary asked, grabbing one of the handles on my book bag so I didn't have to lug the whole load myself.

"You mean little Jessup?" Mary's youngest brother, Jessup, was three and a half years to his nephew Franklin's six months.

"Sure do. That boy plays with baby Franklin like they're brothers."

"I suppose that means your sister April's old enough to be a mama to her own brother."

"Ma has a niece who's two years older than her."

"Really?"

"That's right. You know Ma's the youngest of twelve children?" I nodded. She added, "Well, her oldest brother, Alvin, had a daughter two years before Ma was born."

"Now that'd be peculiar."

"Indeed."

We walked on swinging the bag between us. All that talk about the strange ways of families made me ask, "Is your family as plum crazy about money as mine is these days?"

"You mean flying into a tizzy if you so much as spread an extra dab of butter on your bread? Going on about how much every little thing costs? That kind of crazy?"

"The very same."

"Been living that way since Pa lost his job at the mine. Where have you been living?"

"In a house with only one child, before last fall."

Mary smiled real big. "Welcome to the Great Depression."

Seemed like they could come up with a far better word than *great* for a time when near about the whole country found itself stretching a dime to cover the same ground as a dollar.

Turning my mind to money-saving ideas, I only got about as far as a toad spits when I noticed Peter Roubidoux standing on the rock in the schoolyard looking like some crazed politician rallying a crowd to vote his way. All the kids gathered around the rock, staring up at him like he was the resurrection of the Kingfish himself. Lord knows the world didn't need another Huey Long. In my way of thinking, Harper could've done without the first Peter Roubidoux. He always talked trash about Mama, so I didn't exactly rush right up there to hear what had him carrying on.

"Them Yampells are coming down here to build themselves a factory. My aunt Chessie heard tell of the very letter that told our mayor they'd be coming down to break ground on May seventeenth." Peter went all out in his politician imitation—swinging his arms around, shouting his face red, and lying through his crooked teeth.

Heard tell, my eye. Peter tried to fool us into thinking his aunt just happened to hear about that letter. But we all knew Chessie Roubidoux read other people's mail as if it were the daily paper. If the devil made himself a postmistress, she'd be Miss Chessie's identical twin.

"What will they be making?" Henry Baker asked. Once a foreman for the Journiettes, Henry's papa wore the soles off his shoes near about every month, traipsing across the parish, making his living as a fix-it man.

"It'll be a cannery," Peter shouted. "They're looking to depend on sweet potatoes. The Journiettes are turning their fields over to sweet potatoes, and them Yampells will be canning 'em up."

"When they going to start hiring?" Teddy Carroll asked from the back. In any crowd that gathers in Harper you're sure to find Teddy Carroll and Peter's papa, Eliah, in the back. Those two are nearly giants. If Teddy stood on Eliah's shoulders, he could pick apples off a tree without a ladder.

"Letter said they'd be hiring builders by next week and people to work in the cannery by early July."

Kids slapped their hands together with a "hot damn" and started shouting and carrying on about having jobs and food on the table. I heard Missy LaFavor craving after a nice juicy ham for Christmas. Made ham sound like some divine dessert only rich folks could afford. The whole of it thinned my heart. I'd have to think about the risks of getting wet if I saw that girl drowning, but nobody should live a life without meat on their table.

I saw Mrs. Owens standing on the school steps rubbing her weak eyes. She must've seen what Peter had in mind next. He pulled that crowd up quiet when he yelled, "And that letter said they'll be needing lots of folks, so many they could hire kids as young as thirteen."

Boys and girls started shouting things like, "They'd hire me!" and "I could get me a job!"

"That's my thinking!" Peter punched the air with a clenched fist. "Who needs school when you can get yourself a job?"

Just like with any other politician, the crowd clapped and cheered like Peter brought that company to Louisiana himself. But those kids didn't figure on the weight that rides on change. It's like standing on the edge of a lake on a day so hot your brains have started to fry in your head. You see a big old wave coming in and think how body good it'd feel to have that water wash over you. When that wave comes in, you're washed clean over and dragged across the beach. You're cooled off all right, but you haven't settled anywhere near where you expected to end up. That's change for you. And I'd had enough changes in my life to sense a hurricane brewing with those Yampells and their company. All Peter's talk sounded too much like lies coated in promises. I just hoped the promise of jobs didn't mean the town of Harper would be swept away in the storm the truth would bring.

Rings and Rumors

alf the older kids didn't even bother to go into the schoolhouse that morning. They figured on it being a waste of their time since they'd be hired on by the Yampells soon enough. The classroom looked as empty as it did come harvest time. Mrs. Owens went on about how an education will take you farther than a factory door if you work your way to graduation. But the way kids swam around in their seats like tadpoles flung out of water told me they didn't hear a sound she made. Near about everyone had their mind on that factory and the money it'd bring in.

I had myself a job already. The libraries took all the time I had to give. Maybe Papa could take on a job there. But I hated to think on him canning up sweet potatoes with the machines clanking and grinding around him. A man of thinking ways, he'd be frazzled to a sorry state in no time by all that clatter. The whole cannery situation did seem like a God tailored answer to the wish I'd made for Lara just that morning.

Still and all, the whole idea of it settled into my heart like a piece of broken glass—in some ways, smooth and comforting, but from another angle, it cut deep. Made me kind of shaky, and I had to wonder what scared me so. Did I fear kids would get their hands smashed in the machines like the young folks working in the mills I read about? Where would the Yampells be building such a place? Did some folks run the risk of losing their homes? Would the place make the town stink? Why, Wicksville had a cannery, and that place smelled like someone'd thrown a whole pile of shoes on a fire.

Sitting there, staring at the empty blackboard, hearing Mrs. Owens's voice bobbing through my mind but never landing, I realized what scared me so. The town of Harper would become somewhere different. That factory would wash over the place like a regular old tidal wave—crushing and crashing its way through everything I'd known since we came here when I was three. I'd been losing my life a piece at a time for a long as I could remember—first Bennie, then Mama. Along came Lara who shifted my house around until I didn't recognize it anymore. Now the town of Harper was sinking into sand.

I turned to Mary, who sat beside me like a young lady in church, all stiff and proper with her pretty dress and fancy curls. I felt like a self-pitying fool. Of course Harper would change. Every living thing did. Without it, we'd die.

Knowing the truth didn't make it any easier to swallow. I near about put new ruts into the road with the way I dragged my feet to the libraries. Mrs. Linzy and a few other ladies from town stood on the stoop of the East Library waiting for me to let them in for their Wednesday Bible study. The way those ladies chattered, their Bibles clutched to their chests, I knew they didn't have the Lord on their minds—they were gossiping.

"Nissa, did you hear the news?" Mrs. Jeffery Journiette shouted.

"About the cannery?"

"Yes!" Mrs. Linzy sounded as gleeful as if she'd just gotten a dozen silk stockings. "Isn't it wonderful?"

"Peter Roubidoux got kids so excited about it at school, they didn't even bother to go inside. They're all fixing to ditch their books and get to work," I said as I filed through the cluster of women to unlock the door.

"I know," Mrs. Journiette said. "Folks have been coming out to our place looking to be hired on. How we got figured into it all, only heaven knows."

Opening the door to let folks in, I answered, "Peter heard tell that your folks will be growing the sweet potatoes they're fixing on canning."

Mrs. Journiette's face filled with the panicked look of shock. Once again, being married to the youngest of the Journiette clan had proven to be a deep embarrassment. The Journiette's had to be the most powerful family in the parish, hands down, but being the youngest in the family meant Jeffery was the last to know what the family had planned. That poor woman must've felt like the last peach left on the tree.

"I see." She smiled, but shame filled her eyes.

No one else paid her any mind. They rushed into the East Library chattering away about this and that like a gaggle of geese headed to water. I left them in the east reading room and headed to the West Library.

I didn't need to open that door. I'd given the key to Miss Rinnie Lee months back. I never turned a key over to Mrs. Linzy because I figured she'd be nose deep into my records faster than a bear can find honey in a tree.

"Afternoon, Nissa," Miss Rinnie Lee called to me as I came in. That woman looked like God had told her she'd been awarded the first seat in heaven—all beaming eyes and smiles.

"What is it?" I asked, heart glad to hear something truly happy.

"Looky here." She held out her left hand, and a gold band glistened on her finger. "Straight from his mama's hand to mine."

"Ira finally did it!" I shouted.

The room behind us fell silent. The ladies on the other side had gone into listening mode. Rinnie Lee and I covered our mouths to laugh at their nosy ears, then shuffled into the kitchen to keep our news private. I hugged Rinnie Lee. We laughed again, the happiness like an electric current zapping between us.

Ira Simmons had been sweet on Rinnie Lee for years, but he didn't feel proper about marrying her until he had some property of his own. That Christmas, he'd bought himself a little piece of land and come spring, he'd started to build on it. Now that the roof had all its shingles, he'd finally proposed.

"Isn't it grand? We'll have the wedding in our own house." Rinnie Lee hugged herself over the thought of it.

"Makes me want to cry," I said, but I'd already started.

Rinnie Lee got all teary too. "Look at us!" She slapped my arm. "You'd think we'd been cutting up a bushel of onions."

"When's it going to be?"

"Juneteenth."

"Just right." I gave her hand a squeeze. "You let me know what I can do."

"You can tell your mama to get her fanny down here. I want her gardening, painting, and sewing hands at the ready!"

"Yes sirree!" Pride filled my heart near to bursting, thinking on what a beautiful wedding my mama could give her friends. God had granted her many gifts—she could near about make a rose rise up out of rock, paint a flower so real you could smell it, and make a dress fit for church from curtains.

Taking a deep breath, I said, "This here is genuine good news. Puts all that cannery nonsense to shame."

Rinnie Lee shook her head, "It sure don't, Nissa girl. We need that cannery in here."

"I suppose." As we spoke, we set to work reshelving books without so much as a word on the subject.

"Why do you think I have so much time to help you out?" She slipped a book into its place. "My cafe's near about deserted. Nobody has so much as a spare nickel for a bowl of gumbo filé."

"Maybe they'll build the factory on this side of the tracks and folks'll walk on over to your place on their lunch break."

"Then there'd be no convincing me I hadn't died and gone to heaven." Of course, it would be a heaven sent miracle if many white folks showed up in the Crocked Gator. Mama, Papa, and I had eaten there for most of my life before I even thought on the idea that few other white folks came in.

The thought of the cafe full to brimming with folks of every color sent me and Rinnie Lee to laughing. A loud rap against the common wall pulled us up short.

Mrs. Linzy's muffled voice came through, saying, "Have reverence for prayer!"

If she could see through walls, cranky old Mrs. Linzy

would've gotten a glimpse of the ugly look we threw at her. I said, "I'd like to show her some reverence."

"Nissa." Rinnie Lee nudged me. "Going up North done put the fire of God in you."

I'd gone up to live with Mama in Chicago the year before, seen how city folks lived. But more important, I'd learned how to say my mind. I'd always done it with Mama and Papa but not with folks in town. Now I let my tongue wag to anybody. Lara said it wasn't respectful. As I see it, you've got to earn respect in this here world, and growing older doesn't get you anything but more wrinkles and stiffer joints. If a body wants my respect, they've got to live a good life. No Bible-studying bigot is going to earn a thing from me.

"You know, I almost wish God did baptize adults in fire— burn all the ugliness away. I'm sure Mrs. Linzy's got something nice hidden away from view."

"Of course she does." Rinnie Lee nodded, pretending to be serious, but she burst out laughing. I joined her, and we had to rush into the kitchen to avoid Mrs. Linzy's wrath. Yet another moment being half a child made special.

That night at supper talk of the cannery filled the kitchen. Lara spoke of how she'd get herself a job—maybe picking out the potatoes too poor to can.

Papa looked as though he might float right out of his chair as he talked about how he could get some work for the newspaper, printing up notices and advertisements. He'd found a way to do something that fit him just fine. The cannery couldn't be all venom if it lifted some of the worry off Papa. That idea made me feel a little less heavy on the inside.

Seeing Lily Maeve spreading smooshed peas around her high

chair tray made me ask, "What about Lily Maeve?" I gave her pea-coated hand a shake. She looked at me as if I planned to take it away.

"They'll have three shifts at the factory," Lara said. "I can work the evening shift, so Ivar will be home to look after our girl here." She took her napkin, dipped a corner into her glass of tea, then started to wipe up Lily's hands and face.

Papa watched, his eyes glazed with happiness.

Sitting there, I was struck by the idea that just such a conversation might be filling the kitchen of many a house in Harper. In a strange kind of way I felt my mind drifting out, settling into all those houses, hearing the voices, smelling the food, knowing all of Harper had been touched by the same thing in one day. Made me feel at home.

The Truth in Pieces

The building of the cannery brought everything out into the open—big old machinery to dig up the ground, more lumber, bricks, and shingles than it takes to build a church, and a whole mess of strangers from up North to supervise the project. And when they staked out the building site behind the new part of town, the lies started sprouting up like flowers from bulbs no one recalled planting.

A few years back, when folks voted on putting in a new sewer, Mayor Kinley said the surveyors he brought in swore on the fact that we couldn't rebuild the sewer in town on account of it being so close to the swampy ground to the west. Instead, he had a sewer put in north of town, and folks like Lara's people built houses out there. But when that cannery moved in and set up right behind that cluster of houses, everyone knew the truth. Good old Mayor Kinley had put that sewer in to bring a factory into town. No one seemed to be bothered by the lie. I figured they'd change their minds when they discovered the toilets at work could do more than flush once a day without giving in like ours did in town.

But no one paid any mind to such things because the Northerners coming in had them turned against themselves. Everyone wanted good jobs, but they didn't like the fact that they had to take them from the Yankee carpetbaggers who came to Harper in their shiny automobiles and moving trucks. Those northern folks built new fancy houses out by the factory and bought up all the finest property around town. Eloise Simpson even sold the Moonshine Palace. That's what folks called the big old place she built on moonshine money. After she turned that grand old place over to the Yampells themselves, Eloise moved into her family's house with her sister Ruth.

Yes sirree, those folks from up North had everyone buzzing. The Minkies said they wandered around the mercantile laughing at our food and yammering about how they couldn't buy things like silk stockings, toothpaste, bananas, and something called tampons. The train station filled up with their crates of fancy fixings. When folks went to call and welcome them to town, the Yankees inspected the dishes they brought as if they expected to be poisoned by our food. Rinnie Lee told me how she met up with one of the Yankees at the post office, and darn if that lady didn't stop her, saying, "Excuse me, miss."

"Yes, ma'am?"

"Would you be interested in a job cleaning house?" She smiled real big like someone advertising for tooth powder. "I haven't found anyone yet."

"No, ma'am," Rinnie Lee answered all cool, knowing she'd rather make that woman a cup of coffee filled with cayenne pepper. "I find running my own cafe mighty satisfying."

"Oh." The lady stammered and fumbled with her handkerchief, saying, "I'm truly sorry." Then she rushed right out of there, and Rinnie Lee had herself a laugh over that silly white woman from up North who figured all black folks had to do with their lives was clean up after white folks.

And did those people complain about the heat. You'd think they'd never seen a hot day in their lives, the way they fanned themselves and pulled at their clothes. Heavens, they sweat more than a woman having a baby, saying things like, "This heat's enough to boil your blood" and "Doesn't it ever cool off around here?" Heck, summer hadn't even started yet.

But I didn't pay much mind to any of those silly Northerners because someone much more important showed up—my mama. That morning I sat in the garden with Lily Maeve, picking blossom after blossom to show to the little one. Of course, she preferred eating the flowers over looking at them, so I spent a lot of my time plucking petals out of her mouth. In fact, I was finger fishing for a rose petal when Mama walked in through the back gate—her britches rolled up to her knees, no shoes on. Her hair hung over one shoulder in a tangled curly mess.

"Morning, Nissa!" Mama always arrived acting like she'd never left.

"Mama!" Yanking my finger out of Lily's mouth, I jumped to my feet to give her a hug.

Mama took a step back in pure shock. "Child!"

"What?" I looked myself over, trying to figure out what caught her so.

Circling around me, Mama said, "You been standing out in the rain?" She laughed. "You're sprouting up like a fern under a dripping gutter."

Turning, I came face-to-face with Mama. Sure enough, I'd grown right up to meet her in the eye. "I'm as tall as you."

"Such a smart girl."

"Mama." I shook my head.

She hugged me, rocking me back and forth like she thought I might have grown roots and she needed to break me free.

Pulling back, I said, "What are you doing here?"

Mama bent down to Lily Maeve, who'd taken to eating a pansy.

"They're bitter," Mama said, pulling the flower out by the stem. "Here." She reached over to the honeysuckle along the garden wall. "This is a bit sweeter." She handed the flower to Lily Maeve, who chomped away.

"Mama."

"She's gonna eat anything she gets her hands on. Why not feed her something tasty?"

"Mama, you didn't tell me what you're doing here."

"I don't suppose 'breathing' will suit you as an answer?"

Folding my arms one over the other, I said, "No."

"Well then, I heard tell about this new factory and thought I'd see how things are coming along." Scooping Lily Maeve off the ground, Mama headed for the back door. Lily Maeve bobbed along, acting like she'd known Mama every day of her life.

"Really?" I followed, feeling like Mama dropped tiny bits of truth as she traveled along, letting me know as little as possible without actually lying.

"Where's your papa?" she asked, stepping inside the house.

"In his study, of course."

"And Lara?"

"Napping."

"Smart woman, your mama." She tapped Lily Maeve's nose. Starting up the stairs, she added, "Then again, Ivar wouldn't settle for no dummy."

Keeping in step with Mama, I asked, "How'd you hear about the factory?"

"In a letter I got from Ira."

"Ira Simmons writes you letters?" The shock of it pinched my heart. Time was when folks in town thought Mama and Ira had run off together. They'd been friends for years—the sort of thing black men and white women didn't do in Harper. Then again, Mama never did anything the way folks around town were accustomed to. I knew about their friendship and all, but it still took me by surprise that they wrote to each other. It just seemed like a sweetheart thing to do.

"What part of that do you find so surprising, Nissa?" Lily Maeve took to playing with Mama's lips.

"All of it, I guess."

Mama scrunched up her brow like she didn't see the mystery in it. "He writes. I write. We live half a country away from each other. What did you expect him to do? Send me wooden tablets with chiseled messages?"

In Ira's hands a twig could become a hummingbird. He had the God given talent to build any old thing a person would care to have. "No, I guess I just didn't know your friendship included letter writing."

"Uh-huh." Mama nodded, looking as confused as ever. She figured her way of doing things made all the sense in the world. "Well, I don't know any other way to keep in touch with a man who doesn't live near a phone."

Knocking on Papa's study door, she said, "Ivar, come out here and feed this baby of yours before she eats the entire garden."

"Heirah?" Papa opened the door so fast, I wondered if he'd flown across the room to do it.

"Ivar." Mama smiled.

Papa squinted in confusion. "What brings you down here all of the sudden?"

"Sudden, my eye." Mama handed Lily Maeve to Papa, then turned back to the stairs. "I've been on a train so long, I feel like the ground's still rumbling beneath me. Let's get that baby some food."

Mama moved around the kitchen like it still belonged to her, making Lily Maeve some grits with applesauce, telling us the whole of the truth she'd been spilling out a bit at a time.

"Come to find out Mr. Keller never paid all his bills from turning the hotel over to apartments," Mama said, putting water on to boil.

Mr. Keller was the fella who hired Mama to help him start a theater in the old dining room of that converted hotel. Mama built sets, painted backdrops, sewed costumes, and even fixed backed-up toilets—she was a whole workforce rolled up into one person. Time was when Mr. Carroll went north to help out, but he came home again once he became a grandpa.

Papa kept pace with Mama's story as if he'd been up in Chicago himself, saying, "And he ran into trouble with the people he should've been paying."

"That's right." Mama didn't stop, she kept right on flitting here and there to fix the food, never turning our way. Everyone there except Lily Maeve knew what that meant. Mama had bad news. You could feel the weight of it in the air.

Papa sighed. "And they took the building as payment."

"Uh-huh." Mama's answer came out all jagged, like her sadness had cut it up.

"I'm so sorry, Heirah."

"Thank you, Ivar," she whispered, stirring water.

I didn't know what to say. The shock of it all had frozen me from the inside. Mama's backdrops made whole worlds open up behind the actors. You expected smoke to billow out of her chimneys, birds to fly out of her trees, and the warmth of sunlight to stream out of her sunrises. When I saw Mama working in the theater, it looked to me like God had built the job just for her.

My heart started to thaw and got all quivery, so I asked, "And they closed the theater?"

Mama nodded but didn't turn my way.

The next question just slipped out of me. "And you came down here for a job in the factory?"

The quick trill of laughter spilling out of Mama's mouth made both Papa and me jump with surprise. Lily Maeve just answered with a laugh of her own.

"Heavens no." Mama spun around to lean against the sink, her face red from tears but her eyes bright with laughter. "I wouldn't work in a cannery even if they offered me the chance to can up old Chessie Roubidoux."

That idea made Papa and me laugh. We all knew Chessie spread lies about Mama near to as often as she read other people's mail.

"Then do tell," Papa said, catching his breath. "What's next?"

"Well, Ira and Rinnie Lee's wedding for one thing," Mama said, getting the applesauce out of the icebox.

"Uh-huh." I echoed Papa.

"And with all these folks coming south, they'll be needing furniture."

"You're going to help Ira build furniture?" I asked. With Ira's help, Mama had built me the most beautiful dresser, with carved and painted flowers spread over the whole thing, as if they'd grown out of the wood.

Mama's face got long and pale, like I'd caught her in a lie. "Not exactly."

Papa went stiff. "Then what, Heirah?" His voice sounded just as rigid.

"After the theater closed, I got another job."

"Doing what?" I asked.

When Mama left Harper to find her happiness, she tried her hand at all sorts of jobs—waitressing, rock picking, typing. Heck, she even branded a cow while cooking at a ranch.

Sitting down at the table, Mama said, "The new owner gave us all a month to pay his higher rent or move out, so I had to find a job and another place to live. This antique store down the street had a room for rent. I figured I could help fix up old furniture and have the room in trade."

When she lived with us, Mama used the bedroom across the hall from the kitchen as a keeping room—a place for all the broken things she found. She kept them there until she found a way to rebuild them as something new—an old dresser became a wedding trunk for my Aunt Sarah, a rocking chair joined up with a jam cupboard to become a cradle for my dolls, and our old dishes were ground up to cover a new thread box for Grandma Dee. Mama could make any old thing into something new and magical.

"I went in and tried to convince the fella there that he'd make a lot of money from my talents, but he didn't believe me. Said his man studied under some European furniture maker to learn how to rebuild antiques. He didn't need any Southern

Sally coming in there turning his furniture into country trash."

I could see Mama standing in that shop, her face as still as a pond at dawn, but her mind just grinding up a good answer. "You mean like this dresser here?" She'd walked over to a beat-up old thing that looked like it'd been pulled up into a tornado then spat out.

"That's a recent acquisition," the man said in his out-of-a-book way of talking.

"And how much is it?"

"It's not for sale, miss. I just bought it to rebuild."

"How much will you get for it when it's all finished?"

"At least fifty dollars. It's a fine piece."

"And if I got you sixty?"

He laughed. "You?" He pointed at her with the pencil he held. "You couldn't make that dresser worth more than the five dollars I paid for it."

"Then we have a deal." Mama slapped down the five dollars and started carting that dresser away. She had it wedged in the half-open door by the time the store owner got around the counter to come stop her. Mama created such a ruckus, people on the street started to stop and stare, so he just let her go.

Mama went to the library, checked out a book on the fancy French furniture that's all painted up with flowers and such. She stripped and sanded down that dresser, fixed its drawers, repaired the legs, gave it new handles, and painted that thing up pretty enough for a queen. When Mama brought the dresser in, the man accused her of buying it from another dealer.

Mama pointed to the paint on her clothes, saying, "You see this blue here? Don't it look just like this flower? I painted this dresser, and I'll take the profit from it too."

The man went back to his counter in a huff, but that dresser sold two days later for sixty-three dollars. Mama had herself a new job. Just like that.

As Mama finished her story, the boiling water started spitting over the edge of the pan, so she got up to tend to it. Papa and I stared at each other over the table. Mama could convince the pope to become a Protestant, we were sure of it.

"And?" Papa sounded uncertain, like he knew he had to keep digging to find the rest of the truth. "How does that bring you down here?"

"Well," Mama said, pouring the grits into the water, "that fancy repairman didn't take too well to working with a woman."

I smirked at the "good riddance" hidden between Mama's words.

"And?" Papa dropped "and"s like they primed Mama's story-telling pump.

"That fella got himself another job. Daniel, the shop's owner, couldn't find himself a suitable replacement. Half the country's out of work, and he couldn't track down anybody that met his standards." Mama gave a snort of disgust, then said, "As I figured it, if anyone can build furniture, it's Ira Simmons, so I told Daniel to head on down this way. I couldn't haul Ira up to Chicago so close to his wedding. 'Sides, old Daniel is set on raking in antebellum antiques at half their value up North." Mama laughed, knowing he wouldn't find much in Harper that Ira hadn't built himself.

"I see." Papa nodded.

He seemed satisfied, but a suspicion rose up inside of me. She never called Mr. Keller by his given name. Why'd she call this man Daniel? And why'd she bring him back to Harper? Couldn't she just as well bring a piece of Ira's work with her when she went back north? Mama still hadn't laid the truth out plain. If her life of late had been a dress, we'd only seen the bodice as yet, and I feared the skirts had a romance hiding in the folds. Papa had his Lara. Did Mama have a new man called Daniel? The idea of it made my blood fill with the heat of anger. Mama had walked out on her husband and her daughter, broke off a promise she'd made before God to love and cherish one man until death parted them. She had no right to take up with another man.

The Gathering Storm

*L*ike fires set from lightning strikes during a dry heat, tiny storms started all over town that spring. Folks got to talking about the citified fella, named Daniel Thurston, who'd started selling furniture out of Ira Simmons's barn. What white man would set up shop with a black man? Who did he expect to be buying his fancy furniture, with its crushed velvet seats and gilded edges?

The Yampells set folks to rumbling when they hired Henry Baker's papa to be their building supervisor, and Mr. Baker turned around and picked Ira Simmons and Jacob Carroll to be his foremen. People began to suspect those Yampells of partiality to Yankees and colored folk, knowing Mr. Baker came from Ohio and Mary's papa came from Pennsylvania. Then there was Ira. Everyone knew he could build a house fit for heaven, but they didn't like the idea of part of the building crew being black. No white man would work for Ira, and he'd been put in charge of all the framework and roofing, while Mr. Carroll had been hired on as mason and electrician. Of course Mr. Baker would head up the plumbing crew, but no one took kindly to the notion of all those colored folks snatching up jobs that could go to white folks. That fact had white folks gathering at the Thibodeaux brothers' feed store every night, causing a holy ruckus while the sensible people sat out on the back porch of the Crocked Gator to celebrate their good fortune with some iced tea and lemon cookies.

Now, the storm brewing at our place started as a low rumble in my own heart when I suspected Mama of courting Daniel Thurston, but it whipped into a proper gale when Lara woke up to find Mama in her house feeding her baby.

Papa had gone over to the newspaper office to set some type, so it was just us girls at home when Lara walked into the kitchen kind of blurry eyed and stumbly. Then she saw Mama, and it looked like someone had splashed a bucket of water in her face, the way she snapped back and stared open eyed. "What on earth are you doing here?"

"Feeding your child," Mama answered, spinning a spoon around in the air until Lily Maeve opened her mouth.

"I see." Lara leaned onto the counter with one hand and put the other on her hip like some kind of human teapot. "And were you planning on giving her an evening bath as well? Maybe singing her a lullaby before bed?"

Mama's voice turned cool as she stirred the grits, saying, "I could do both if they need to be done."

"They do," Lara said, sitting down right next to Lily's high chair so she faced Mama. "By her mother."

"Her father doesn't do such things for her? I find that hard to believe." Mama put her hand on the high chair tray. Lily Maeve played with her fingers, coating them with grits and applesauce.

Lara had her eyes fixed on Mama so hard, you'd think they could've burned Mama's skin. "Indeed, a father should do such things. And her sister, Nissa, reads her books, dresses her, and plays with her until the cows come in. But just where do you think an ex-wife fits into this little family?"

I didn't so much as let the air out of my lungs for fear it would set those two clashing like lightning does with thunder.

"Right in front of you. Sitting not two feet from her own daughter." Mama faced Lara now. I couldn't see her face, but I knew that tone. It had the edge of warning in it—the kind that set your nerves on their sides, made you ready for anything. "And both our daughters are right here, listening. Learning. Now, what do you think they're learning about you?"

"You . . ." Lara swallowed the word and breathed through her mouth like she might start yelling at the drop of a spoon.

"There's a way out of this, Lara. I can stand up and leave the room. You can slide right in here and feed your daughter. She won't be none the wiser. But not my Nissa. You can't slip even the swiftest change in mood past her. You'll have some explaining to do then. Take it from experience." Mama stood up, kissed Lily Maeve on the top of her head, and turned to give me a nod before walking through the kitchen door, then out into the garden.

Lara gave a shuddering sigh, then got up to switch places. Feeding Lily, she made all sorts of silly noises, but they sounded forced and cracked. I had the urge to shout, yell at her for play-ing all nice with Lily when she'd just done a mean awful thing. But what does a baby know of the truth?

Why did Lara always have to get so angry at Mama for being in the house that'd been hers for near to a decade? I asked my way to the answer right there. She didn't want Mama to stake squatter's rights on her life. Lara's house had been Mama's. Her husband had been Mama's. Even her eldest daughter, if you could call me hers. Then there was Lily Maeve, the only thing she could truly claim as her own—not that a person can be claimed in such a way. But still, Lily came from Lara's own blood, and there sat Mama feeding that sweet little thing as if she'd brought that baby into the world herself. Lily certainly seemed to be enjoying herself. That had to sting Lara's heart.

"Mama doesn't want what's yours." I said it slow and clear, but it echoed in my mind like I'd shouted it.

"I know," Lara whispered, shame coating her words. Shaking her head as she fed Lily, she said, "My mind could lay bets on the certainty of it. But when I walked in here and saw Heirah acting like she never stepped a foot out that door, my temper shot my good sense straight to hell."

"Mama has a way of doing that to folks."

Lara actually laughed. "Doesn't she though. I'm going to have to take lessons from your papa on how to keep your mama from setting my heart on fire."

"Good luck with that." I patted her on the shoulder as I headed for the door. "I know it hasn't done me much good."

"Nissa." Lara said my name in a way that made is sound like an invitation to stay.

I stopped. "Yes, Lara?"

"I'm not a quick-tempered fool. Your mama just shakes me up so."

"Don't I know the feeling." I forced a smile, then stepped into the hall.

Mama had gone into the garden, but the idea of going to her

didn't settle right. For the first time since I'd laid eyes on the glove wearing, husband courting Lara Ross, I didn't want to choose sides. Mama had set this storm to brewing when she left Papa. Lara had her reasons for needing to claim a little space of her own. And I knew how soul stretching hard it could be to make a place for yourself against the whirlwind of my mama. I stepped out onto the front porch instead and listened to the faint orchestra of the builders echoing out of the distance.

That music played through each day from dawn to dusk for weeks. We lived our lives to that beat—Mama and Lara calling a truce of silence, sidestepping each other like boxers avoiding the first blow, Papa negotiating printing jobs with the Yampells, Lily Maeve growing, drooling, and laughing through it all. Me, I spent my days in a near to empty schoolhouse and my evenings in the libraries, where the building music made the darn shelves shake.

Mirrors and Angles

What with her wedding coming on and all of Ira's crew eating at the cafe, Rinnie Lee had no time at all to be helping me at the libraries, but that didn't matter to me none. School had let out for the summer. Not to mention the fact that I had a personal goal of never meeting Daniel Thurston for fear of giving in to a murdering rage at the mere sight of him. All told, I enjoyed being elbow deep in too much work at the libraries.

Doing research for painting play backdrops had given Mama a powerful hunger for books. Add that to the fact that she lived in the upstairs of the West Library, and anybody'd understand why she was in some part of the libraries on most days, plopping down in a window or on a bookshelf to read some such thing. She'd call out new facts to me as I reshelved books.

On the Monday before the big wedding Mama had picked herself a spot on top of the history books in the East Library. Rolling over to look down at me, she said, "Did you know women used to take ribs out of their bodies to make their waists no bigger than a darn loaf of bread?"

The idea of it made me short of breath. "No, and I guess I could've gone a long way without knowing such an awful thing."

"Well, keep it in mind when you start thinking on shaving your legs and wearing stockings, high heels, and face powder. Be happy with the body God gave you, or let the devil make you miserable. It's your choice." Mama turned on her back and crossed her legs, bobbing her bare foot in the air.

"You're preaching to the wrong girl there, Mama." I went to the checkout desk for more books. "You ought to be having that talk with Mary Carroll."

"Mary Carroll?" Mama shouted. "I would if I could find the child. I passed some lunatic on the street the other day talking like some lemon-eating bird to Gary Journiette. That girl was all trussed up in a fancy dress and toe-pinching shoes."

"That was Mary."

"Does her mother even recognize her?"

I laughed. "I suppose she finds it an improvement. She used to say hanging out with me put the boy into Mary."

"Boy, my eye. Where's it say only boys can wear britches? Heck, didn't Jesus go around in a dress?"

Mama always saw things in the wildest ways—like the world around her only existed when she needed it for something. She didn't see color in a person's skin unless I burned mine by sitting out too long and she needed to rub it with alcohol. She figured women had a right to their own room, the clothes of their choosing, and any darn job they cared to try. And those ideas sure didn't come from her own mama and papa. Why, Grandma Dee always said God raised Mama before she was born. She came into this world with such ideas. And as a child, I took them as my own without giving it a second thought.

"So you think men should be able to wear dresses?" I said, climbing the ladder below Mama. "How would Papa look in that green dress you made last year?"

"Fine enough, except for the fact green makes that pale skin of his take on the color." Mama flopped her hand in the air like the ladies in the mercantile do when they get to gossiping.

"He'd probably look quite nice in navy blue."

"Indeed." Mama couldn't hold it in any longer—a giggle sputtered out of her. I joined her. We both laughed until we squealed.

"Oh, child, I do love you." Mama slipped around like a snake on the narrow top of those bookcases and kissed me full on the mouth.

"Mama! You could fall!"

"Fall?" Mama gripped the edges and set to swaying. "Not on shelves built by my daughter!"

The shelves leaned toward me with a groan. In my mind's eye, I saw myself buried under a pile of books. "Mama!"

She let go and stayed still until the shelf stopped moving. "I didn't mean to scare you, Nissa. You are such a cautious child." Mama would try hang gliding with a sheet and broom if she lived near a mountain—that woman didn't know fear existed.

"You're just crazy." I stomped back down the ladder.

Mama leaned over the edge, looking like a little girl that'd been caught in the act of devilment. "Nissa?"

"Yes, Mama?"

"Do you have any idea how often I thank God for your speciality?"

I felt a fluttering tickle in my heart. "What?"

"You. How you just plow your own furrow." She fishtailed her hand through the air to show me. "You're not your papa, not your mama, nothing like Lara, just you."

"Thanks, Mama."

"Only stating the truth up here. Only stating the truth."

I had my eyes on Mama as she lay back to read her book, so I didn't see anyone come in through the west door. I near about ran right into some girl I'd never seen.

"Good golly, sorry about that." I fumbled my way backward to give her some room.

"No matter." She laughed. Holding out her hand, she said, "I'm Carolivia Simpson, Rinnie Lee's cousin. I'm here for the wedding. She sent me over to lend you a hand."

"You don't say." I shook her hand.

"That's right." Carolivia nodded, her long braids sliding over her shoulders.

"Nice to meet you, Carolivia. I'm Nissa Bergen."

"That's what I figured. Cousin Rinnie said to look for myself in white skin."

"Excuse me?" I laughed.

She pointed to her legs. "A tall girl in britches with her hair in braids who loves books, fishing, and alligator jambalaya."

"Indeed." A spark lit inside me—that hot charge of friendship I'd known with Mary before womanhood swallowed it up.

Stumbling over my own feet, I turned around to point up to Mama. "This here is my mama, Heirah Rae Russell." It still seemed odd to call Mama by her papa's name, but she'd given her married name over to Lara.

Mama peered over the shelf, all smiles, shouting, "Howdy!"

It was Carolivia's turn to jump. You'd think she'd seen a bat fly out of the rafters, the way she screamed. Patting her chest, she said, "My stars. There's a woman up there."

Mama put her foot in the air and tapped the ceiling. "Come to think of it, I should paint some stars up here."

To protect the speciality of my twelfth birthday present, I warned Mama, "No you don't. The only night sky ceiling in Harper is in my bedroom, and I plan to keep it that way."

"Aye-aye, Captain Nissa!" Mama shouted down.

Carolivia stared at us like we were two monkeys speaking Norwegian in a tree house. I said to her, "Don't expect to get used to her neither. Mama's about as predictable as a cornered bear."

Mama said, "Speak for yourself."

"I think she was," Carolivia said, and we all laughed. After a minute, she asked, "What you want me to do? I came to work. I aim to do it."

"Yes, ma'am." I headed into the shelves and Carolivia followed me.

Just then, Chessie Roubidoux came in the east door, shouting, "Afternoon, all!" as if Mama, Carolivia, and I weren't the only three other people in the place.

Carolivia turned as if she wanted to go help, but I took her hand, more to defend her from Miss Chessie than anything else. "You don't want to go over there."

"Oh." She kind of bowed her head. "That's right. Cousin Rinnie told me you don't allowed coloreds over in the front. I'll stay right here till you get back."

A knife to the heart might've felt gentler than that one line of words. I never so much as hinted at the idea that no one could pass the invisible line between the east and west libraries, but no one ever did. Nor did they ever tell me about seeing the East Library as the front. Here I thought I'd built those libraries up equal.

My head sort of rolled in a nod as I drifted toward Miss Chessie, knowing I didn't want her to go flapping her gums at Carolivia. Almost as if I could shut Carolivia's comment away, I closed the door behind me.

As I came forward, Miss Chessie said, "Now, Nissa, I need a book on canneries. I'm fixing to get me a job when they open up, and I need all the know-how I can get."

"The cannery?" I mumbled. "You thinking on taking an evening shift job for after the post office closes?" I hated the idea of Lara having to work with Chessie only a fraction as much as I loathed the thought of making folks feel like I'd given them second best, but it still seemed like an awful possibility for Lara to have to endure.

"No, child." Miss Chessie's chirpy voice turned gravelly. "I've left my position with the post office. I'm moving on to better things." Her smile looked like she'd wiped it clean off one of them gargoyles they have hanging off the buildings in Chicago— all stone and evil.

"Sounds fine, Miss Chessie." I nodded, half expecting Mama to drop in a few cutting words. Chessie Roubidoux had always done her best to paint mama into a demon in the eyes of the town. I figured Mama'd have a lot to say about Miss Chessie losing her job. Nothing short of being fired could've driven Miss Chessie away from the direct line to the lives of Harper that her job had always been. But Mama didn't so much as stir as I showed Miss Chessie to the special collection on canneries I had set up in the yellow room upstairs that'd once been Lara's own bedroom.

Coming down the stairs, I had trouble knowing if my feet touched solid ground. My body had gone all light. Mama stood at the bottom of the stairs looking up at me with that sad face she took on when I fell and hurt myself bad enough to bleed.

"Nissa." She put her hand on my shoulder. It felt good and heavy. I knew I wouldn't fly off then. "You've got to know you built a hall of mirrors here."

"Huh?" My mind had grown so muddled, her words almost sounded like gibberish.

"Every one thing in this building can be seen from a thousand different angles."

"I don't understand, Mama."

Mama held up her book. "Take this here. To a man who doesn't read, it's a waste of paper or a paperweight." She smiled a little. "To me, it's a story of folks gone sick in the head trying to fit some crazy fool's idea of pretty. Now, to that fool, it's a testament to how beauty can change a person for the better. And this list can go on forever."

"What's that got to do with the libraries?"

"To Lara, this place'll always be her house full of books." She pointed up the stairs. "To folks like old Chessie, this here door"—she patted the East Library door—"means she's got a right to call herself a lady while she thinks less of folks like your new friend back there. But you and I know the real people with a place in your heart and a weight in your soul, come in through your kitchen door, straight into the place where you live. They don't waste their time with no front door or silly parlor."

What Mama said could've stood as the truth, but my mind still spun and I felt dirty shameful through and through. She shook me by the shoulder. "You hear me, Nissa?"

"Yes, Mama." I wandered back to the West Library, begging God to forgive me and to give me the strength to do what was right. I found Carolivia reshelving books. My voice had grown thin and gotten lost. It took me quite a time to find it again, so I could say, "Carolivia."

"Uh-huh." She didn't look my way.

"You can go in any part of this library you have a mind to."

She looked at me, her face still. "That why you have two libraries? Send our folks to the back door?"

"No." I took a deep breath to try to keep myself from shaking, but it didn't do me any good. "There are two libraries because a preacher in these parts tried to have just one church, and they burned that church to the ground with him and his family in it."

"So you're protecting your hide."

"And yours. If you'd walked into that room today, Chessie Roubidoux would've made your life worth about a cup full of spit." From somewhere, I felt a growing sense of steadiness that pushed my words out before my mind had the chance to get a good hold on them. "And if I'd known how to chop this here building in half and put a front door on both sides, I would have. But then we'd have had a North and a South Library. I don't see how that's much different. If you ask me, you're taking directions to mean a lot more than they do."

Putting the book she held on top of a shelf, she said, "That mean I can check out any book in this here library?"

"The book of your choosing."

"I don't have to tell you what I want so you can go get it, even if I don't find it on the shelves in here?" She waved her hand in the air to indicate the room we stood in.

Most times if someone from the West Library wanted a book that I'd shelved on the other side, I went over to fetch it myself to avoid an unnecessary battle. But just then, I figured Carolivia saw such a battle from a different angle than I did, so I said, "That's right."

"Then I'll just go through that door there and find myself a book."

For a second I thought to remind her of Miss Chessie, but then I saw everything for the test it was. Did I have the strength to face whatever came from doing the right thing? God willing, I would, so I said a quick prayer in my head, then told Carolivia, "Happy hunting."

She walked through the door marked, THIS WAY TO THE EAST HARPER LIBRARY. And I felt my soul go with her.

Friends and Foes

*T*ried not to watch as Carolivia walked among the shelves on the east side. But it seemed like my eyes had been anchored to her by a fishing line no one could see. They kept drifting back to her long black fingers with the bright white nails, touching each spine. They didn't shake. She didn't hurry. Stepping slow and sure, she marked out her territory like a farmer measuring his field for planting.

Meanwhile my heart squirmed like a snake on a hot skillet. I couldn't keep my hands still if I nailed them to the desk. What did I think would happen? Chessie Roubidoux would come down the stairs, take one glaring look, then march into town to scare up a burning party? Not likely. But I still felt as if I stood on the edge of a cliff in a mighty strong wind.

Mama sat on top of the shelves, her knees pulled up to her chest, smiling down on Carolivia with admiring eyes. Mama had a keen respect for strength and I feared it. Mama had called it right when she said I wasn't like her or Papa. In that regard, my own furrow ran deep and yellow—fit to bury a coward like me.

As I tried to busy myself with paperwork Carolivia walked up to the desk and handed me a copy of *Treasure Island*—the very copy Peter Roubidoux had donated to the libraries. It gave me chills of pleasure to sign Peter's book out to Carolivia. One on account of the fact that I'd done the right thing and the ceiling hadn't burst into flames. Another because creepy old Peter had not only donated the book, but he'd tried to convince me it wasn't a book fit for girls. As I signed the book out to Carolivia, I felt like saying, "So there, Roubidouxs." But I just handed the book back to Carolivia with a smile, then said, "Good choice."

She nodded, saying, "Thank you." A smile spread over her face as she said, "So now what do we have to do around here?"

Hoping I'd passed the test and put us two back on the road to friendship, I said, "Truth is, I've been working since early morning and there isn't much left to do. I say we go fishing instead."

Carolivia slapped her book in excitement. "You bring the poles and I'll hunt up the grubs. My mama wouldn't let me pack my pole for the train ride."

"Don't go taking the fun out of it. We'll go grubbing together."

"Sounds dandy."

Shuffling my paperwork into piles, I called out, "You mind guarding the fort, Mama?"

"It'd be my pleasure," Mama said into her book.

"Nice to meet you, Miss Russell," Carolivia said as we stepped out the front door.

"Bye, girls!"

"See you soon, Mama." I still got a thrill out of being able to say such a thing again.

Heading to the road, I couldn't help but feel the coldness of a stare. Did Chessie Roubidoux see us out the window? I didn't have the courage to check over my shoulder. I just led Carolivia down the road and into town, praying my little show of strength would remain a secret.

As I came down Main Street with a string of fish that evening, I caught sight of Mary sitting out on her front porch with Gary Journiette, the redhead whose prickly hair made him look like he had fiery grass growing out of his head. Mrs. Carroll sat on the other end of the porch pretending to be mending.

"That you, Nissa?" Mary called.

"Sure enough." I walked up to the porch, my fish dripping onto the steps.

"Been fishing, I see." Mary stared at my fish as if I'd gone to the mercantile and bought a pound of blueberry saltwater taffy just to dangle in front of her. That girl prized that candy like a cow loves its salt.

"Yep."

"All by yourself?" Mary smiled, but it looked as painted on as the color of her lips.

The shame of going without her filled me up like smoke, nearly making me choke. "No, Rinnie Lee's cousin came in for the wedding. She helped me up at the libraries, so I took her fishing."

"They're biting good!" Gary shouted, missing the whole point of the conversation, as usual.

"That they are, Gary." I shook my head.

Mary said, "I can help you at the library, Nissa. All you have to do is ask."

Time was when Mary would've met me at my back door to walk to the libraries together. But now she had her heart riding on Gary Journiette, a boy who still hadn't passed the sixth-grade exams at sixteen.

"Oh, I know, Mary. I just didn't want to take you away from good old Gary here." I kicked Gary in the toe. He laughed like some little boy gone all bashful.

Mrs. Carroll looked at me over her sewing glasses, saying, "You better get those fish home before they ripen, Nissa."

"Yes, ma'am." I knew Mrs. Carroll meant to get me off her porch before I started something with Gary. He and I had been known to do more than go toe-to-toe on occasion.

"Have a good night now," Gary shouted, glad to be rid of me.

"'Night, all!" I waved as I walked in front of the porch.

Cutting between the Carrolls' and Mr. Beaurigard's, I whispered to Mary, "See you."

She nodded and gave me a half smile.

Lara fried up the fish with onions, pepper, and just a splash of apple vinegar. After supper Papa sat at the kitchen table with his jobs-for-hire poster spread out and weighed down with things like the salt shaker and the sugar bowl. Underneath him, Lily Maeve sat on a blanket banging measuring cups against the table leg.

I spent my time stuffing a printed advertisement into envelopes with letters from the Yampells talking up their hiring dates, shifts, and positions.

Papa mumbled to himself as he shifted words around. Sewing up a torn dress, Lara sang little tunes to Lily Maeve, who just banged all the harder, like she had a mind to keep the beat but didn't know how. Just when I thought I'd burst from the constant clanking and the paper cuts in everything from my fingers to my tongue, a knock came at the back door.

"I'll get it!" I jumped up. No one else even seemed to notice, so I ran into the hall.

Mary looked gray behind the screen door. "Hi, Nissa."

"Mary."

"Gary's gone now, so I thought I'd come over."

"I'm helping Papa with a mailing."

"But you've got to hear this."

"What?"

"Chessie Roubidoux got fired today!"

I felt like saying, "I know." But the excitement in her voice pulled me in like a fish on a hook. "Do tell." I stepped outside. She linked her arm in mine, and we headed to the benches under the cherry tree.

"The Yampells have this fella named Carpenter who does all their business in town. I saw him at the mercantile just yesterday. I went over to buy Ma some more thread. And he came in, all shiny shoes and fancy hat, and walked right up to Mr. Minkie to say he wanted to set up a charge account for the employees at the cannery. They'd charge items and the Yampells would pay the bill—a kind of paycheck-by-barter sort of thing. Mr. Minkie didn't go for the idea at all. He just stood there, turning that ruby ring of his, until Mr. Carpenter offered him two hundred dollars in advance. Can you imagine that? Two hundred dollars?"

"That's enough for a new car."

"Indeed." Mary slapped the bench to agree. "Anyhow, I heard how Mr. Carpenter fired Miss Chessie today."

"I'd give at least a kidney to have been there."

"Gary's sister Bella saw the whole thing."

"Do tell."

We hunched together as Mary told her tale. She gave all the right details to let it play out in my mind like a picture show. Miss Chessie had been standing behind the counter sorting through the mail, slipping some letters into a crack in the counter on the sly. Later on, with the help of a little steam, she'd open those letters and read them before dropping them into the proper boxes. The teapot was always on to boil in the post office, but no one ever saw Miss Chessie drink a cup of tea.

Mr. Carpenter came in. He tipped his hat to little Bella, who still had her hand in her mailbox. She'd never seen a man in a full suit outside of church before. Walking right up to the counter, he pulled an opened envelope out of the inside pocket of his suit coat. He said, "Miss Roubidoux, it has come to our attention that you've been reading our official correspondence."

"Pardon me?" Miss Chessie looked as if he'd asked her the color of her underpants.

Setting the envelope on the counter, Mr. Carpenter said, "This letter was opened before it was delivered. In testament to that fact, Mr. Yampell sealed this envelope with clear wax and not a drop of it remains."

"And what gives you the right to accuse me of such an act?" Miss Chessie put her hands over her secret stash of letters. "There must be a dozen mail folks between here and your office up North."

"He posted this letter from his house on Marvel Street, Miss Roubidoux. Since you pick that mail up on your way to work, you're the only postal worker to have touched this letter."

Miss Chessie froze as if Mr. Carpenter had painted her on to a canvas.

"Since you're so fond of reading letters, you might like reading this one." He slid a letter across the counter, then turned to leave, taking real slow steps toward the door.

Miss Chessie fumbled to open the letter then mumbled as she read though it—dropping words like "postmaster" and "testimony." She looked up, all pale and shaky. "I'm fired?"

Racing around the counter, she rushed to get in front of Mr. Carpenter. "You can't have me fired. I've been working here for nearly thirty years."

"That's about twenty-nine too long, Miss Roubidoux."

Miss Chessie screamed her face red as he walked out. Bella got so scared, she started to cry. That made Miss Chessie notice her. She grabbed ahold of Bella and told that girl she'd boil her like a pig if she told a soul what had just happened. That poor girl ran home wet in face and dress. Old Chessie had honest to goodness scared the pee right out of her.

I didn't know whether to laugh or curse. That nosy beast of a woman had finally met an enemy she couldn't defeat, then she turned around and terrified a little girl into a flight of fear. Even the Yampells couldn't contain Chessie's evil ways.

"Can you believe it?" Mary shook her head. "I wonder who they'll get to replace her."

"I don't know, but Miss Chessie plans to get a job at the cannery." That reminded me of Lara's plan to get a job there. But what did Lara need with such a noisy old place if she could get herself a better job? "Lara could take Chessie's job. That'd keep her out of the cannery."

"Now, there's an idea." Mary nodded. "But I know April plans on applying for the post office job."

"Your sister doesn't like cleaning rooms at the hotel?"

"The cleaning is fine, she just hates working for Mr. Cassell. That man could find fault with God. Besides, he doesn't pay enough to keep food in the cupboard, even with Winston's job at the feed store."

I couldn't help thinking that the Yampells might be taking a nice bite out of Mr. Cassell's pride pie in due time. He walked around in clothes fit for church every day, showing off his old-time watch and ruby ring like they made him somebody. That man acted like he owned Harper on account of the fact that he hosted all the elections, the town dances, and the fancy wedding receptions.

I put my hand out. "May the right woman get the job." We shook on it, but it felt kind of odd that I didn't side with April right off. I'd known April for ages. Mary and I had been best friends for just as long. Lara came into our lives under three years before that night, and already I felt the need to side with her.

"Mary Carroll!" Mrs. Carroll shouted from their back door.

"I better go."

"See you soon," I said as she went through the back gate. I doubted I would.

But the sad thing was, I didn't seem to mind. I just turned around to go tell Lara my idea for a new job as the next post-mistress of Harper.

Old-Fashioned and Peculiar

"Postmistress?" Bathing Lily Maeve in the sink, Lara looked at me like I'd suggested she run for governor.

"Why not?"

"Because I have enough trouble walking in your mama's wake. I don't care to step into Chessie Roubidoux's shadow, thank you very much."

I'd never thought on the fact that the person who took over Chessie's job would have to deal with that dragon woman's wrath. I didn't fancy squaring off with the likes of her myself, but still, it didn't seem right that she held all that power. "You could show folks how a postmistress is supposed to do her job. You'd be so fine at it after a time, no one would even remember Chessie Roubidoux except to spit on the times she'd read their mail and spread their news around town."

Lara laughed. "Sure thing, Nissa. I'll just step right over there and get that job. Don't you think Chessie's going to be naming her successor? Why, Chessie's the closest thing to the Kingfish we got around here. She'll name who she wants to take the job."

Sometimes it hurt to see how different Lara was from Mama. Now, if Chessie stood in the way of something Mama really wanted, she'd just plow right through that bony, evil woman. I recalled a time when Mama and I had gone over to the mercantile for a look-see at what had come in on the train. Miss Chessie arrived before us. She stood right next to Mrs. Minkie, watching every little thing that woman took out of a box.

Buying a fistful of black licorice, Mama hopped up onto the counter in front of the old sorting boxes they used for mail before they had a separate post office. I climbed up there with her. She handed me a piece of licorice, then took a pulling bite of another, saying, "So what's new, Miss Agnes?"

Mrs. Minkie glared at Mama. She didn't take to women who sat on counters. "You'll have to wait and see, Heirah Rae, just like the rest of the folks around here."

"Just like that patient Chessie Roubidoux."

That time Mama got a double-barreled shotgun of a stare from those two women. I bit my licorice so I wouldn't laugh.

"You want some candy?" Mama offered them her licorice.

They got all grumbly and huffy and set back to unpacking. Mama and I started making up stories on the things Mrs. Minkie took out of the box. The percolating coffeepots should've been shipped to a Baton Rouge hotel, but the place burned clean to the ground after a young lady writing a letter to her lover got startled by her papa and knocked her lantern to the floor. The yards of blue fabric with the white doves would have become curtains for the governor's mansion if it weren't for the fact that doves made his wife think of magicians, and those fellas scared her worse than ghost stories in a graveyard. Mr. Minkie even stopped dusting the shelves to have a listen to our stories. He folded his hands on the counter, his old ruby ring all glinty in the sunlight.

But those ladies sneered and clucked their tongues at us, saying things like, "A grown woman should have better things to do with her time." Meaning Mama. When those ladies got to talking about what a person shouldn't be doing, they were almost always meaning Mama.

Then Mrs. Minkie pulled out a small wooden crate. Miss Chessie asked, "What's that, Agnes?"

"Not sure."

The ladies went over to a counter to have a look inside. Mama just started guessing. "Frog hearts for voodoo rituals!"

"Stop that!" Mrs. Minkie shouted. But I laughed.

"Misshipped glass eyeballs meant for the veterans' hospital in New Orleans!"

"That's enough." Mrs. Minkie got so flustered, she couldn't even open the box.

Mr. Minkie laughed as Miss Chessie yelled, "Oh, I just can't wait." She popped that box open and pulled out the most beautiful crystal angel, all flowing and smooth, like water frozen into glass.

"How fine." Miss Chessie held it up in the sunlight, and it cast a rainbow onto the dusty wooden floor. Mrs. Minkie went all gap mouthed.

Mama hopped down onto the floor and started over to them, saying, "I'll take that."

"What?" Miss Chessie hugged it to her chest. "Who's to say I'm not buying this here angel?"

"Well, I just did. I said, I'll take it."

Mrs. Minkie said, "You can't have it on credit, Heirah Rae. I'll only sell it for cash." She smiled.

"All right. How much is it?" Mama tilted her head, waiting. "Nissa, get your legs ready to run. I need you to fetch some money." Mama never carried her money. She kept it in a drawer in the kitchen.

Hopping down, I said, "Ready, Mama."

Taking the angel, Mrs. Minkie looked at Miss Chessie, then said to Mama, "Five dollars."

Mama didn't even take a deep breath. Five dollars could've put food on our table for a week. "You got five dollars, Chessie?"

"Well . . .," Miss Chessie stammered.

"Go fetch the money out of the drawer, Nissa."

I hightailed it out of there as Miss Chessie tried to hide the fact she couldn't afford no five-dollar statue. Mama only had a dollar twenty-five in that drawer. I brought all the money straight to her. Out of breath, I dumped it into her open hand. She closed it right quick before anyone could see what she had, then said, "I'm waiting, Chessie. I need to see your five dollars."

"I'm selling it, Heirah Rae." Mrs. Minkie straightened her shoulders.

"And I'm waiting for her to pay for it."

You could see the anger brewing in Miss Chessie's face, the redness bubbling up like froth in a pot of beets. "I don't have it."

"You got a buck and a quarter?" Mama held out her open palm.

Chessie glared at her.

Mama slapped the money on the counter. "I'll take it for a buck and a quarter." She snatched that angel out of Mrs. Minkie's hand and marched out of the mercantile. Those owly ladies didn't even try to stop her. Mr. Minkie nodded to her, saying, "Miss Heirah."

The price tag on that angel said $1.75. Mama had bested Chessie Roubidoux and saved fifty cents in the bargain.

But now Lara didn't even have the strength to apply for Miss Chessie's job. She made me feel shameful.

"The way I see it, you're the one giving Miss Chessie the power to name her successor. If you're too scared to even apply, then what'd keep her from doing whatever she wants?"

Lara lifted Lily Maeve out of the water and wrapped her with a towel. Hugging Lily Maeve to her chest, she turned to face me. "Nissa Marie Bergen, I'll never get used to that mouth of yours."

"My mouth?"

"I see the face of a child when I look at you, but the words coming out of your mouth are too old. You talk to me like I'm your younger sister, not your stepmother."

Well, the words that filled my mind at the moment went something like, "Don't act so foolish if you don't want me to treat you that way," but I pressed my tongue to the roof of my mouth to keep those old words from escaping. Then I said, "I don't mean disrespect, Lara. I'm just telling you what I think."

"Then your thoughts are disrespectful." She walked out of the room.

I felt like she'd dropped me into steaming hot bathwater. My temper could have made that water boil. Disrespectful? Who calls the truth disrespect? A fool, that's who. And why such a person deserved my respect, I'll never know.

I marched upstairs, knowing talking to Lara would do me as much good as a ripped umbrella in a rainstorm. I went straight to Papa's study. Knocking, I heard Papa say, "Come in."

He sat at the desk, figuring out the bills. I felt bad for disturbing him, knowing how money weighed on him.

"Is something wrong, Nissa?"

Turning to face the door, I said, "It can wait."

Papa flipped his ledger book closed. "My mama used to say, 'One tear costs your soul more than a pound of gold.' By that idea, I figure bills aren't worth my time if there's something bothering you."

"Your mama said that?" Papa didn't talk about Grandma Nissa much. But everything I knew about her made me love her. She died when Papa was small, before he and his family even left Norway. But I loved how she grew a garden, made muffins in the shape of little men, and sang songs.

Papa nodded. "She always had such great things to say. When it came to worrying, she always said the same blessing over us kids, 'Be mindful of angels and stay on course.'"

I remembered Papa saying the same thing to me one morning. Papa believed everybody had a host of angels watching over them, leading them along. Now I knew he got that idea from his mama. Made me feel warm inside, like I knew her somehow.

Papa had a way of making you feel like you could turn your soul inside out—he'd see everything and still love you. I could tell him most anything, so I told him everything that had just happened between me and Lara down in the kitchen.

Papa took a deep breath, then held it for a second. Pushing his chair back, he patted his thigh. "You aren't too big to sit in your papa's lap, are you?"

"No, sir." I climbed into his chair. It did feel kind of awkward, like I might hurt him if I moved around too much. Leaning into his chest, my face next to his, I remembered how, not long ago, I was small enough to put my head over his heart and listen to his words echo in his chest.

"You've got to remember, Lara grew up in a family like most everyone else's. At the table kids didn't speak unless spoken to. Parents didn't talk about their plans. They just announced them. Folks didn't talk about feelings much. Her mama certainly didn't sit out on the roof to look at stars or paint murals on ceilings. Lara's not used to a life like ours."

"I won't get mad at her for living an old-fashioned kind of life if she won't get all dragony over mine."

"Nissa, Lara isn't old-fashioned." Papa hugged me. "We're plumb strange."

I laughed. Papa joined me. "Laugh all you care to, Neesay, but it's God's honest truth. Except for eating, sleeping, and the other regulars of life, your mama and I haven't taught you how to do one thing like other folks."

I kissed him on the cheek. "And I thank you for it."

He gave me a push. "Off with you then."

"What should I do about Lara?"

Papa raised his eyebrows. "Give her some room to settle in to our way of living. She's still adjusting to being a mama."

"Thanks, Papa." I opened the door.

"And, Nissa."

"Yes, Papa?"

"If it matters, I agree with you on the postmistress thing."

"It matters." I smiled.

From all the rumors, awful looks, and nasty comments, I knew Mama did things her own way, but I guess I never did figure on how much I'd learned from her and how different that made me from other folks. Thinking on what Papa said, I realized Lara came from a different place than I did, like another country with odd customs. Papa's family used to cut holes in the ice and go swimming. In Norway that's a normal sort of thing to do. In Harper folks'd figure you'd gone soft in the head for doing such a thing. In the same way I acted peculiar to Lara, and she acted peculiar to me. Now we had to find neutral territory. That'd be a trick.

As I settled into bed that night, I heard Papa and Lara arguing to beat a practicing band. Years back I might have had my ear up to their bedroom wall, but I'd shed that disrespectful habit. Only trouble was, eavesdropping is near to impossible to avoid on a spring night when all the doors and windows hung open and voices travel like wind. Papa was trying to convince Lara to apply for the job. She kept coming back at him with the same old-fashioned ideas—Miss Chessie would haunt her like a murdered ghost. Plus she didn't like the thought of giving in to my way of thinking after we'd fought. She said it undermined her authority. Like she had any real authority over me in the first place. Normal or not, Lara was a coward.

$\mathcal{G}$rowing $\mathcal{T}$ruths

*L*ara and I peacefully ignored each other for a few days. Mama became as scarce as rosebuds in a snowy winter. I kept my mouth shut and my mind turned to solving the problem of making two libraries into one. Come Friday, Mama woke me up by tapping on my bedroom window. My room overlooked the garden from the upstairs. Used to be that the only one who walked the stone garden wall to come through my window was Mary Carroll. She came in that way to avoid meeting up with Papa. Mrs. Carroll didn't take to my wild boyish ways, and Papa didn't take to all the courting-related things Mary passed on from her sister, April. Now Mama used that garden wall to avoid running into Lara. Folks say fences make better neighbors, but they never did say anything about how handy they can be in a family like ours.

"Morning." Mama stepped into the room looking like a dog covered in paint had shook itself out all over her. Giving me a kiss on the check, she asked, "Hungry for some breakfast?" She drew a bulky napkin out of her pocket, from the blue-and-white check of it, I knew she'd brought me something from the Crocked Gator. Flipping the edges back, she revealed baking powder biscuits slathered with blackberry jam.

"My stomach's always ready for some of Rinnie Lee's jam and biscuits." I grabbed for a biscuit.

Mama pulled her hand away. "Good, then get dressed and we'll have our breakfast on the way to the shop."

"Shop?" I asked, slipping out of my nightgown.

"Yup." Mama sat in the window seat and started eating a biscuit as I got dressed. "Daniel thinks barns are only fit for cows and pigs, so he bought the old Henfield place. You know, where they used to have a dry goods store until the Minkies put them out of business."

"A shop, here in town?" My mouth went as dry as if I'd eaten a dozen biscuits with no milk.

"That's right." Mama licked her lips.

"As in, for good?" I asked, dropping my britches around my ankles.

"Shops aren't a seasonal thing, Nissa. You open them and hope they stay open. It's the general idea of the thing."

"But what about his shop in Chicago?"

"He's having everything shipped here. Said he could buy that place for the price of half a year's rent up North." Mama frowned. "Nissa, don't you see what this means? I can live here in Harper."

"I know!" I near about shouted. "And you told me you'd rather live in hell than come back here." The whole idea of Mama turning back on her word had me revved up like a race car. I could've gone a mile in a minute flat.

"I can't change my mind?"

"Change your mind? Like you thought you wanted to marry a man and raise a family, but you changed your mind?" Mama could shift with the wind, but she always forgot who might get blown over in the process.

As she stood, I felt the heat of her anger like burning sunlight on my face. "Leaving here had nothing to do with changing my mind about wanting to raise you."

"How could you raise me if you never saw me again?" I actually yelled at my mama. She and I were engaged in an all-out shouting match. Somewhere deep inside me, the swirly charge of a thrill spun up. I was standing my ground with Heirah Rae Russell, the hurricane of Harper. "When you walked out that door, you never planned on coming back! Did you?"

Mama stared at me, her jaw jutting back and forth like she chewed on words of stone. "No, I didn't." Her voice lowered and went smooth like it sailed on nothing but clean air. "I left this house thinking I had set you free."

Mama took my mind and flipped it clean over. "Free?"

"That's right, so you could be free. And look here, now you're free enough to stab me with my own sins. And I know they're sins, Nissa." Licking a tear off her cheek, she said, "I broke your heart to give it a chance to grow. Not in my shadow. But in your own light."

Even one tear in the corner of Mama's eye was enough to make me cry. I was near to blubbering already. "What are you saying, Mama?"

"I'm saying, from morning to night, you were my girl. My heart's music." She touched my hair and I leaned my head into her hand. "We fit together like a petal to a stem. And you were always trying so hard to make me happy. I depended on you for my happiness, in fact. Felt like I'd started to bring you down inside me so I'd have that happy feeling forever. But that ain't true happiness. That's love turned crooked. And I knew it'd eat you up in the end. I had to leave before I swallowed you whole."

As a child I ran home from school nearly every day because I couldn't stand to be away from Mama any longer. When she left, it felt as if I'd been skinned from the inside. It wasn't until Mama brought me back into her life that I realized I didn't know where my own self began. She spoke truth and it broke my heart all over again. Mama had left for me. But not just for me. She had to leave to find herself in something other than motherhood. She came back as a better mama in the end.

I hugged her until it felt like our bones met. "I love you, Mama."

Mama patted me on the back, saying, "Good, then you'll help me finish up my wedding present for Ira and Rinnie Lee."

Wiping my face, I asked, "So that's why you wanted me to go to the shop?"

"Yep." She gave me a push. "Now get dressed. I'm not taking any half-naked child of mine to meet Daniel."

"Must I?" I sniffled, pulling up my britches. I didn't feel up to adding yet another member to our odd family just yet.

"He doesn't bite, and except on rare occasions, he's gotten his drooling under control. I can't say much for his barking, though. He can't seem to hold himself back. Especially under a full moon."

"Mama." I laughed at her.

"Well, what do you expect, child? Shovel nonsense over your shoulder and some of it's sure to fall on your head."

A knock on the door made us both jump. "Who is it?" we called together.

"It's me," came Papa's reply.

"Just a minute," I said, scrambling for a shirt.

"He's coming to see if there are any survivors," Mama whispered with a laugh. "I'll wait for you in the alley."

She ducked out onto the wall as I said, "Come in, Papa."

He looked pale as he walked in. "Everything all right?"

"It is now."

Papa cleared his throat. "I've never heard you yell like that, Nissa."

"Remind you of Mama?"

Dropping onto my bed, he nodded. The disappointment in his face made me feel the grit of dirt on my nerves.

I sat down next to him. "Wish I had something soothing to say, Papa, but Mama lit a fire in me only yelling could put out."

He gripped my knee, saying, "You watch those fires, Nissa, because when they get out of control, there'll be no one who can rescue you."

One time, Mama let her anger take her over, and she hauled off and hit Papa square in the jar. The idea of hurting someone I loved like that made my soul shrink up in my body. "I hear you, Papa." I squeezed his hand.

"Good." He smiled, the light in it warming me right up. "Your mama thinking on staying here in Harper?"

"Did you listen in?"

He laughed. "Nissa, folks probably heard the two of you clear to the Crocked Gator."

I bowed my head in embarrassment. He hugged me and rocked a little. "Don't worry, Nissa. Ira told me that Daniel fella has opened up shop in the old dry goods store."

"That's right."

Papa raised his eyebrows and started to wring his hands.
"Lara and Heirah in the same town year-round. I'll never sleep."

We both laughed.

Papa caught his breath, then sighed, saying, "So you're mad
at your mama for coming back?"

"I guess." I shrugged. The new truths of her leaving still hadn't
fully settled in my mind yet. "You know, part of it is that Mama
just does whatever she wants, whenever she wants, and she always
seems to find a way to make it all right in the end."

"Darn annoying, isn't it?"

"Darn straight."

Papa stared off for a minute like he took a short trip to the
past. "Makes you want to paint her face with stinging nettle paste
while she's sleeping, doesn't it?"

"No." I laughed. "You've thought of such a thing?"

Papa smiled. "More than once."

"And she probably deserved it too."

"More than once."

Laughing, I said, "I better go, Papa. Mama's waiting out back."

"All right then." Papa kissed my cheek. "Don't let your mama
twist your soul up. Just be mindful of angels and stay on course."

"Yes, Papa." I stood up, kissed him on the forehead, then
headed out the window. "Have a good day."

"You too." Papa waved.

I ran down the length of the wall. For a flash of time I
thought I could jump down into the alley and land as smooth as
a cat. I looked down and saw Mama looking like I held her heart
in my hand and my jumping would squeeze the life right out of
it. Then I knew foolishness had taken my mind. I turned around
and lowered myself down.

"You had me thinking you'd been taking flying lessons for a minute there."

"No, Mama, I'll leave that to you."

I'd grown up believing my mama could fly—just jump off a riverbank and sail on over to the other side in a chase to catch a butterfly. Nowadays I knew her to be the type of woman who'd take lessons to become a pilot if she had a mind to. It's odd how your parents grow in your mind's eye just as you do in theirs—half of it is a shift in your way of seeing things; the other half is changes inside the soul—the kind of growth only the careful eye can see.

Doing the Right Thing

Getting within eyesight of the old dry goods store showed me why Mama'd arrived covered in paint. That place had gone gray from wind and rain a dog's lifetime ago. Now it stood at the end of the alley as bright and colorful as Mama's own garden. She'd painted the building white, then sent flowery vines around each corner and along every edge. Made the whole street look different, like the other buildings sunk a little in shame.

Mama stepped right up the newly sanded and stained steps. "Come on in, Nissa girl, see what we've done inside. But keep to the middle. The floors aren't all dry yet."

Following Mama through the front door I realized they'd sanded, stained, or polished every living inch of that place. "When'd you do all this?"

Mama turned toward me but kept walking to the back of the shop. "Don't you remember? Ira can't sleep when he's nervous."

"You stayed up all night?"

"For nearly three days running." Mama raised up on her toes. "Makes me feel all hollow, like I just might disappear."

Stepping into the back room we came into a maze of old furniture. A tall man weaved his way among all the pieces, inspecting each one. He had that stiff look you only see in old gray pictures of long-dead relatives nobody can remember. I suspected he was the type to starch and iron his shirts and change them when he sweat too much. That man wouldn't last a summer down South.

"Oh, Miss Russell." The flatness of his voice told me he was a Yankee. He looked as sour faced as a fella who'd bit into a lemon thinking it was an orange. "I need your help. There is a couple looking to furnish the house they just bought, and we don't have a thing on the floor."

Mama bounced on her feet and made the floorboards creak. "Sounds like it's got plenty of weight on it."

He ground his teeth together. "I won't bring customers into my storeroom."

"Then you won't be selling much furniture. Only the center aisle's dry."

"You promised me this place would be ready."

"You're inventing things again, Daniel." Mama yawned.

"Will you please call me Mr. Thurston? Why is that so hard to remember?"

"Seems to me you're the one with the memory problem. I told you we'd have the place ready for the shipment from Chicago. This stuff's from Shreveport. And if you can find somebody who can work faster than me and Ira, well then you've left this earth and won't need to worry about any silly showroom."

Listening to Mama verbally mop the floor with prissy old

Mr. Thurston near about made me laugh out loud. Here I'd been thinking she was sweet on him when she couldn't stand the air he breathed. Once again I'd gone and applied normal ideas to Mama's way of thinking and doing. Most folks might figure a woman uses a man's calling name when they're more than friendly, but not Mama. She calls a man like Daniel Thurston by his first name because she knows he's all wrapped up inside manners and rules. Mama hates manners for their own sake, so she'd call such a man Daniel.

"All right, fine, fine." He shook his head as he walked around a table. "I suppose we could sweep in here and dust."

"There are plenty of boys around who'd be happy to earn a nickel."

"I'm not going to drag some unknown child in off the street, Miss Russell. They'll need references."

"References?" Mama laughed. "Mister, I know every man, woman, and child in this here town, and you wouldn't find a two of them who'd know what in the Sam Hill a reference is. Just stand out on the porch and call down to the Gator for some kids looking for work."

Mr. Thurston puckered up his lips like he wanted to cinch in his words. Then he blurted out, "Who is *this* child?"

"This child is the town's librarian and my daughter, Miss Bergen."

I knew if I opened my mouth I'd laugh, so I just waved.

He mumbled and nodded back.

"Come on, Nissa girl, we've got a wedding present to finish." As we headed to the workroom Mr. Thurston busied himself with polishing furniture. All the wood looked like dark glass already. Except, of course, for Mama's row of furniture. Her stuff looked like stained glass, with all its carved and painted flowers.

Mama's present stood in the center of the workroom. If it had been a stained-glass window, it would've been the big one behind the alter. Brick by carved-in brick, Mama had turned a Hoosier cabinet into a brick wall with a trellis covered in blue trumpet morning glories.

"What do you need me for? This looks good enough to fool a gardener."

"Thank you kindly." Mama bowed. "But the truth is, if I stick my nose over one more can of finish, I'd faint dead away."

"You want me to brush on the finish for you?"

"If you don't mind." Walking up to a bag of rags, Mama slid down to the floor. "I'll just rest up here for a bit."

"You got me out of bed to put a top coat on this cabinet here so you could go to sleep?"

"I promise not to snore." Mama crossed her legs and closed her eyes, then mumbled, "Thank you, Nissa."

"You're welcome, Mama."

I turned to my work with a few complaints under my breath. But as I started tossing and turning my thoughts, I uncovered a whole new idea. If Mama didn't fancy Mr. Thurston, why'd she drag him all the way down to Harper? The townsfolk had nearly leeched the life right out of Mama with their crooked-for-straight ways—saying Mama was evil for socializing with black folks when it's a sin to hate a person for the color of their skin.

Mama made it sound like she brought Mr. Thurston down so she could keep her job and give Ira some steady work in the bargain, but I couldn't bet on that idea. No, Mama had another reason she kept tucked away from view.

Tossing this problem around in my mind I had the top half

of the cabinet done before I remembered Mama had tricked me into finishing her present. I kept right on going on account of the fact I hadn't thought of a good gift for Ira and Rinnie Lee myself. Finishing off Mama's gift was the least I could do.

I only had the drawer fronts left by the time Ira walked in looking as if he'd missed the door on his own shop and came into Mr. Thurston's instead.

Jumping in front of him like I could block his view of a huge piece of furniture, I said, "Ira, what are you doing here?"

"Don't fret, Nissa. I've seen the cabinet." He rubbed his eyes. "I came to see how Heirah's coming along before I head over to work."

"You've seen it?"

"I gave Heirah the brick to match it up to the fire wall in our kitchen." He yawned. "I had me a nap, so I figured I'd help your mama. But I see she's pulled you into the job. Want some help?"

"Naw." I waved him away with my brush. "Consider it my part of your present."

"All right. Stopped by the Gator for some coffee, and they're just chewing the fat over them Northerners again." He shook his head.

"Everyone keeps talking about the folks from up North like they came down from Mars. Are these people green or something?" I asked, keeping my eye on the surface I brushed over.

Ira laughed. "Not as far as I can tell."

Mama stirred in her sleep, so we fell quiet for a bit, then Ira said in a low voice, "What gets me is how everyone talks about foreigners coming in here and messing with the town."

"Why's that?"

"You name me one family that was here three generations ago."

I thought on his idea. The Carrolls came south when Mary and I were little. Heck, I'd only lived in Harper since just before I turned four. The Roubidouxs moved north from down by Lafayette when Chessie was but a girl. I didn't know a soul who'd been here longer than the Minkies, and they looked as old as trees, but I heard tell they moved here from Vincentville after the war. "Can't think of a one."

"That's right. Harper didn't even have a train stop until 1903, and that's about when the Journiettes came up from New Orleans with all their money and bought up nearly every acre of land the town stands on.

"Rinnie Lee's family is the oldest folks here, and they're the colored line of the old Simpson clan from before they lost all their land to Uncle Sam's avenging taxes and turned to moonshine."

Listening to Ira, I couldn't get over how the place you live is like a friend you've known all your life. I'd walked every dirt filled inch of Harper. I figured I knew the whole parish well enough to draw a map fit for government, but something always came along and surprised me. Friends do that too, like Mary going sweet on old Gary Journiette and turning all womanly, losing all the sass that made her Mary. Tucumsett Parish worked in reverse for me. I always learned things about its past that made me wonder if I'd ever known it at all. Like the church burning shortly after the war. Folks over in Vincentville didn't like the idea of a pastor who'd let the colored folks sit on the same floor as the whites, so they burned the church to the ground—preacher, family, and all. History has it that the killers didn't expect them to be inside the church, but it was a demon evil thing to do even before the murder came into it all.

Now I knew that Harper had no call for screaming at migrating Yankees. No one in town but the Simpsons could trace their blood into its soil. Heck, most folks around the parish probably looked on us as outsiders.

"Nissa?"

"Yup?"

"Sure you're not sleeping over there?"

"Why?"

"I've been trying to ask you what you think of our shop here for a while now. Where'd you wander off to?"

"The past, I guess."

"Don't go there now. The ground's thick with blood and not too much of it is white."

"Ira, did you know that preacher who was burned over in Vincentville?" Ira would've been not much older than me back then.

"Horace Belmin? Sure, I'd seen him around. He and his brother lived on either end of Charleston Road—weighed that road down like it was a rope staked out between two sturdy posts." He nodded, admiring those fellas.

"Did you attend Pastor Belmin's church?"

"Nope."

"He wasn't a Baptist like us?"

"Pastor Belmin was Baptist all right, but not like anybody I'd ever seen. He wore regular clothes on every day of the week. I hear he wore dungarees to the pulpit—said God would receive him in rags if he had a good heart. And you know what that man said?"

In my mind's eye I saw this man behind the pulpit, arms raised to God in blue jeans. The thrill of that kind of freedom tickled me to smiling. "No, what?"

"He said that Jesus was no white skinned, blue eyed, straight haired white man."

"Really?" I dropped my brush right into the pail and came around to hear the rest. I'd always wondered how a Jewish man could look like Christ did in the picture Bibles I'd seen.

"Said he was an ancient Jew with hair as tight curled as mine—probably had brown eyes and dark skin. Pastor Belmin reminded those folks, such a man wouldn't be allowed to sit in the pew next to the white folks."

I leaned in close, almost like it could put me into that church. "What did people do?"

"Left." Ira shook his head. "They couldn't wrap their minds around the idea that Christ could be anything but just like them."

"No black folks were there?"

Ira's answering laugh rattled with sarcasm. "No. Few dared go, thinking they'd be beaten right back out of there. See, Pastor Belmin had that church built on the Vincentville end of Charleston Road—a nice Sunday-morning walk from either town—hoping he'd draw in Harper folks as well as Vincentville folks. But Old Man Journiette sat guard on the Harper end of the road with a gun in his lap. He sent his oldest boy over to sit on the Vincentville end. Nobody even thought on passing those Journiettes if they weren't white."

"Hold on." Ira had my mind spinning. "You mean the same said Charleston Road that crosses Palmer just out yonder?" I pointed.

"Sure enough."

I knew a church on Charleston Road. But it sat on the Harper end. That place had been abandoned for many a year.

Almost every All Hallows' Eve I went to that church with the Carroll children to tell ghost stories. "Does the church on our end of Charleston Road have anything to do with Pastor Belmin?"

"Everything. Pastor Belmin's brother, Davis, tore his house down in that very spot. Folks figured he'd lost his ever-loving mind to grief. I don't know if it was grief or crazed determination, but he built a church just like the one that burned, board for board. I suppose he would've done it on the very ground where the first church stood, but that parcel went to the Journiettes in a flash. Zeph Journiette's place sits there now. In my way of thinking, that church on Charleston Road is the largest tombstone I've ever seen."

I'd told ghost stories on a grave. The sin of it made me go all light.

"Nissa? You all right?"

Sinning and the church made me think of the Carrolls and how they believe folks burn in hell for such things. In a flash I stood in my library, burning. Not for telling any ghost stories but for building two libraries. That Pastor Belmin had it right all along. And he died for it too. Would I?

"What would happen if he built that church today here in Harper? The Pastor Belmin, I mean."

Ira sighed. "The same thing, I'm afraid."

"You wouldn't go?"

"And end up with a belly full from a Journiette rifle? No thank you, Nissa. I'm looking to marry my Rinnie Lee and start ourselves a family."

"Even though it's the right thing to do?" Mama had walked away from all she knew and loved because she felt soul sure that she had to do it. Now, leaving a family is never right, but it turned out to be the best thing. I thought two libraries was best, but now I figured I had to do what was right. Not just for Caro-livia but for everyone. I wanted Jesus to walk free in my library.

"What are you really asking me, Nissa?"

"I'm thinking on making the libraries into one."

Ira stared at something over my shoulder. I followed his eyes. There stood Mama, looking like I held her heart in my hand again. The answer to Mama's return dropped into my head like a rock. She came back because I had her worried. Just like Papa, Mama feared something bad would come of me running the libraries. "It's the right thing, Mama."

Swallowing hard, she said, "That's God's truth there, Nissa. But you remember this, it's a saint who walks God's road straight to death's door by doing the right thing in a place with a soul as twisted up as Harper's. You thinking on becoming a saint, Nissa?"

Saints knew what God would have them do, and even when it meant losing their own life, they did it. That's what Mama meant. History remembered them. Empires fell and their gods faded into myth, but Jesus and the God who sent him to earth are still alive today.

Then again Pastor Belmin never became a saint. Everyone forgot him. Colored folks still had to sit in the balcony of every white church in town. Even Mama didn't go to a black church. I didn't want no saint's glory. I just wanted to see things change for the good just one time. But what made me think I could do any better than Pastor Belmin?

"I want to do the right thing."

Ira put his hand on my shoulder.

Mama nodded, saying, "I know, Nissa. But don't go fitting yourself for any angel's wings just yet. Give yourself a little time to grow into them." Mama forced a laugh, but I could see the fear in her eyes. It gave her a twitch.

"Don't worry, Mama." I smiled. "I won't go trying for any miracles just yet."

She smiled back. I could tell I'd settled Mama a little, but I still felt like I had thorns in my heart. There had to be some way to turn Harper's thinking. My job had to be to find it. And I knew just the person who could help.

Good Sense Gone

ime was when only Mama, Papa, and Mary Carroll came to mind when I thought on getting any help. I went to Mary if I needed advice on how to deal with particular family troubles—things I couldn't ask Papa or Mama about. Like when Papa started casting his eyes on Lara. I had to know if he had courting in mind. Mary had said he'd never court a woman like Lara—she had hairs poking out of her nose. Papa's wedding and Mary's affection for Gary Journiette proved Mary to an unreliable source for advice on such matters.

Mama, on the other hand, gave advice with a bite. She usually spoke the truth like it couldn't hurt a flea on a dead dog's head. Just like she had when Lara walked into the kitchen with Mama sitting there feeding Lily Maeve as if she'd been the one to bring that child into the world.

And Mama didn't shy away from telling herself the truth either. Back when I lived with Mama up North, she told me I had better live my life my own way, because if she had hers, she'd keep me close at hand until I was too old to chew my food. The bite in that truth sunk its teeth into Mama, not me. Takes a lot of courage to tell the truth even when you know it cuts deep, unless you planned on using it like a weapon. Mama did just that at times, but she never meant to. I guess you could say the truth was a weapon Mama kept a secret, even from herself.

But since she'd gotten back to Harper, Mama had been hiding the truth. Sure, it rose up to the surface on occasion, like that morning in my bedroom or when she talked with Lara or Mr. Thurston. But she only used it in self-defense. I couldn't rely on Mama this time—fear held her back.

And Papa, too. All my life he'd been like one of those wise Asian fellas folks travel miles to see. You'd drop a problem in Papa's lap, and he'd think it over, drawing on all the things he knew. Then he'd lay it all out like a problem on a math test, giving you the information you needed but leaving the answer up to you. Sure, I could talk to him about Lara and Mama, but I knew by the way he reacted to news from the libraries that I couldn't go to him about anything related to them. Fear had filled his head with fog.

All my usual sources of wisdom had either been dried up by fear or by the foolishness of romance. I had no idea love could be crippling. So I turned to Carolivia Simpson, a girl who had Mama's way with the truth. I found her on the back porch of the Gator mixing up the wedding cake.

"Morning, Carolivia."

"Nissa." She nodded, measuring out flour.

"What you think I should do about the libraries?"

Carolivia dropped the cup into the mix. "Is this something you want me to decide before or after lunch?"

"What?"

"How am I supposed to know what you should do with the libraries? Who do I look like, W. E. B. Du Bois?"

"Who?"

"Never mind." She shook her head as she fished the cup out. "I just think it's kind of strange that you come over here asking me such complicated questions."

"You're the one who told me I shouldn't keep colored folks out of the other side of the library."

"So don't."

"What do I do if someone sets their mind to burning the place down?"

"Get out of their way, so you don't get burned." Glancing at the back door, she said, "Speaking of which, I've got a pie in the oven."

She headed into the Gator, leaving me to wonder why I ever thought of taking this subject up with a near to perfect stranger in the first place. Staring at the railroad tracks as they stretched off over the horizon, I wondered just what I'd find on the other side.

Carolivia came back with a pie in one hand and a pan of cookies in the other. She set the steaming cherry pie next to me. "These here are from your tree. Your mama gave them to Ira."

"Hope you added plenty of sugar. Those cherries are sour enough to twist your tongue even when they're canned."

"Consider me warned."

I started to think on apologizing for dragging Carolivia into my troubles, but then she said, "Mr. Dupree had him a good idea. Said you should've never even built a colored library. He figures we can build our own library. Make it like we want."

"He told me just that last year." I sighed, feeling guilty for thinking I knew better and building my own. "Don't know why I didn't listen to him."

"You're as stubborn as a horse being dragged to the glue factory."

"Thank you kindly." I forced a smile.

She laughed. "That's a compliment, Nissa Bergen."

"Oh."

"While you're sitting there solving all the problems of Louisiana, why don't you frost those cookies there." She pushed the pan of sugar cookies at me.

In the shape of hearts they looked buttery good. I set to work, saying, "I never kept track of who donated what at the library. I don't know how to give the right books back."

Carolivia stared at me. "Girl, you are color blind, aren't you?"

"Shall I take that as a compliment too?"

"I suppose." She licked her lips. "But you're as ignorant as you are blind."

"Pardon me?"

"Who's W. E. B. Du Bois?"

"I don't know."

"Marcus Garvey?"

"Never heard of him. Is he a writer?"

"William Stillwell?"

"Who are these fellas?"

"How about Harriet Tubman?"

"I know her!" I got so excited, I flipped my knife.

Wiping frosting from her eye, she said, "Good for you. Now, how come it is that I have to know Thomas Jefferson, George

Washington, and all those other powder-headed fellas, and you only know about one of my famous kin?"

"My mama says some of Thomas Jefferson's children are your kin."

"Name me a white man who ran a plantation and didn't end up with children he owned just the same as his cattle."

No matter what I did, said, or thought, Carolivia made me feel as dirty shameful as if I'd just killed somebody with my own two hands. "Carolivia, it ain't like I don't want to know about those people."

"Uh-huh." She kept her eyes on her stirring spoon.

"Can we call a truce?"

"We're not fighting, Nissa. I'm just talking. How about you?"

"I'm listening. I'm listening real good."

"Glad to hear it."

We didn't say much after that. I just frosted. She baked the cake. When I got through, I wished her a good day and left, feeling empty and light, like I could float on home. Walking thataway, I looked down the hill toward the colored part of town. Except for the Crocked Gator, Mr. Thurston's shop, Ira's place, and my one failed piano lesson at Mrs. Villeneuve's, I rarely walked those streets or visited those houses. Funny thing, though, I knew who lived where. The Villeneuve's lived on high ground to the south in the white house with the green shutters and the grand old magnolia. Ira's brother, Leo, lived just down the hill from them in a little place crying out for paint. He spent his time in the garden out back, growing enough food to keep the mercantile in greens and make enough money to send his girl, Saffron, off to college in Mississippi. I heard tell that garden covered more ground than three of Mr. Leo's houses, but I'd never seen it.

Thinking on that very shame, I marched over to the home of Mr. Otis Dupree, hoping he'd be taking his lunch break from his job laying shingles on the factory roof.

His mama, Miss Ursula, sat out on the front porch shucking spring peas, probably from Mr. Leo's garden. "Afternoon, Miss Nissa. What brings you down here?"

"I'm looking for Mr. Dupree."

"He's back at work already. Wants to get done as early as possible. Can't blame him. Lord knows it's hot enough to make your brain sweat, but they're still up there on that roof, just drawing in the heat."

"Maybe I could bring them over some iced tea."

"I'll provide the tea, if you do the walking." Miss Ursula gave a quick glance to her leg. Story is, when she was just a wee child, she didn't move fast enough for an overseer chasing after a slave on the run. That man rode his horse right over her, crushing her leg.

Seeing the stiffness of her leg and the deadness of her twisted foot gave me the chills. I felt a bit like crying, but I jumped up on the porch and said, "You want me to go in and get it?"

"That'd be mighty fine." She smiled. Waving her hand at the screen door, she said, "It's in the icebox. Take the tin cup hanging over the stove."

"Yes, ma'am."

The Dupree house had a big old kitchen with a braided rug in the center that made me think of long nights of family storytelling, can't say why. I got the tea and the cup, then headed outside. "Thank you, Mrs. Dupree."

"Thank you now, Miss Nissa. You tell Otis to bring that pitcher and cup home with him. Don't let him make you walk it all the way back here."

"Yes, ma'am."

I headed toward the tracks. I hadn't done much more than give the factory a passing glance from the West Library windows since they'd started building it. The place gave my nerves the jumps. Now, just past the middle of June, the place looked almost ready to start canning. Long and full of a funny kind of window that looked more like an air vent, the place reminded me of a cow barn. The roof was half shingled, and a whole crew of Ira's men swarmed all over it, shingling away.

Climbing up a ladder on the far end I remembered Mama telling me how she'd worked for an elderly fella who owned a restaurant in Oklahoma. He hired Mama to wait tables, but when a sandstorm took part of the roof off, she tried to repair it. He wouldn't have nothing to do with a woman repairing a roof, so he hired someone else to do the job. From that story I shouldn't have been surprised when all those men looked at me like I'd just walked onto a battlefield.

"Child, what are you doing up here?" Mr. Garver asked me.

"Brought you all some iced tea." Not an easy feat going up a ladder.

"We can come down for that, girl," he said.

"Okay." I backed up toward the ladder.

"Hold up." Ira rushed forward and grabbed the pitcher. "You might as well stay now, Nissa. Backing down a ladder requires both hands for most folks."

"Right." I handed him the cup.

"Your mama send this?" Ira asked.

I nodded toward Mr. Dupree. "Mrs. Dupree did."

"How'd you run into my mama?" Mr. Dupree came over. "Aw, it don't make no never mind, as long as I get a long drink of that tea." He took the pitcher from Ira and poured that tea right into his mouth.

I had to laugh. "You think that's funny?" He smiled at me. Holding out his hammer, he said, "You want to put down a few shingles?"

"Sure." I took the hammer.

It was his turn to laugh. "I was just fooling, child." He grabbed the hammer. "Give me that."

Ira handed the cup off to Mr. Garver, but he kept his eyes on Mr. Dupree. "You should know better than to try such a trick with Heirah's daughter."

"Right." Mr. Dupree nodded. "A fella shouldn't mess with the town librarian."

"That's why I've come."

Ira looked spooked.

"We making too much noise for the ladies to hold their Bible study?" Mr. Garver asked as he got the pitcher from Mr. Dupree.

"No, sir. I came to see if you want your own library."

"Our own library?" Mr. Garver frowned.

"Mr. Dupree, you told me the colored folks in town should have their own library. You think that's what I should do? Give back all the books so you can put them in your own library?"

Mr. Dupree laughed his deep-bellied train whistle of a laugh. All the men gathered for some iced tea joined him. Looking at me, Mr. Dupree asked, "Girl, you came up here to see if we wanted to build ourselves a library?"

"Yes, sir."

"That library's been open, what? Eight months now?"

"Yes, sir."

"You ever seen me in it?"

"No, sir."

"Any of these fellas here been in it?" He waved his arm around.

"Ira and Mr. Garver."

"Really?" Mr. Dupree stared at Ira for a second. "Well, I don't go to no library. Don't intend to. So you can just keep those books where they are." Mr. Dupree turned back to his work, and most of the men did the same.

Ira walked me to the ladder. Nothing I tried made me feel any better. I still felt like I'd sinned my way to some part of hell that looked just like Harper. Ira gripped my shoulder, saying, "Nissa, I know you aim to do right, but don't forget that folks like to make their own decisions."

"Right." I nodded. What an empty-headed thing to do. Of course they didn't want me coming to them saying, "Build yourself a library." What a fool I'd been. I figured I had better start cultivating some good sense before I made every living thing in Harper hate me. "Thank you, Ira."

"Sure enough."

I headed down the ladder, then walked off toward home, hoping I might find some good sense along the way.

Lost and Found

nstead of sense I found Mary Carroll sitting on a bench under our cherry tree. Her legs crossed, her foot flapping in the breeze, I figured she waited on me for an ugly sort of reason. As soon as she saw me, she stood up, then planted her hands on her hips, saying, "I hope you're happy, Nissa Bergen. My sister is going to be working twelve-hour shifts in some noisy old cannery on account of you."

"How do you figure that?" In a funny sort of way, I kind of liked having Mary yell at me, her voice gruff and mean, a hint of the old girl I knew.

"She would've had that postmistress job if it weren't for your silly old stepmother and her college degree."

Mary made going to college sound foolish. But I was the one feeling like I'd shown up at a sack race without a sack. I had no idea Lara had even attended college, let alone had a degree.

"How's that my fault?"

"She wouldn't even have applied for the job if I hadn't told you Miss Chessie got fired."

My heart seized up, knowing what came next.

"That's the last time I tell you anything, Nissa Bergen."

Her words became a bright shining ax, coming straight down on what was left of our friendship. Turning to the house, I said, "Do what suits you, Mary."

She huffed in disgust as she headed for the gate, muttering something about wasting her time with a know-it-all tomboy. She slammed the gate, then stomped on down the alley. Darn if I hadn't already started crying.

I came into the house all wet faced and shaky. Everything I'd done wrong played through my mind like a wicked picture show—over and over—the sound all warbly and loud. Dragging myself off to my bedroom, I flopped into my window seat and kicked the window open.

"Nissa, that you?" Lara called up from the kitchen window.

"Yes, ma'am."

In a bit I heard her clip-clopping up the stairs. She came right into my room, Lily Maeve bouncing on her hip and fiddling with the keys Lara dangled. "I got the job!"

Pulling a shirttail out to wipe my face, I said, "Good for you, Lara."

"Heavens." She put Lily Maeve down on the rug and came to me. "What happened?"

Sighing, I said, "I'm a know-it-all tomboy without a best friend."

"Oh," she laughed. "Don't fret over a silly fight with Mary. You two will patch it up."

"Have you seen that girl lately? She can't be parted from her dear Gary for more than a minute. She's got no time for friends. Besides, she's not too fond of me anymore."

Lara nodded. "That happens sometimes." Sliding down to lean against the wall beneath me, she kicked off a shoe and wiggled her toes at Lily Maeve, saying, "I had a best friend as a child. Rocky Felson."

"Your best friend was a boy?" And I thought Mama's friendship with Ira seemed strange.

"That's right. And if you thought your papa and Mrs. Carroll made friendship hard . . . Huh!" She gave a you-ain't-seen-nothing kind of grunt. "My mother near about made me a prisoner in my own house to try to keep us two apart. But in the end, time did that job for her."

"How so?" I settled in for a good story.

"Rocky started working for the railroad. My father got him the job. He started out running errands on the Baton Rogue line, then he moved up to cleaning engines down there. He came home every weekend. And long about the time we were your age, he started talking up this girl who worked at a cafe across from the rail yard. I got mad at him for spending time with some stranger when he never came around to see me anymore. Sitting in my parlor, he said, 'I'd love to see more of you, Lara. Especially if you showed me things like that girl at the cafe.'

"'Just what do you mean by that, Rocky Felson?'

"He said, 'Give me some sugar.' And then he puckered up his lips like some carrot-crazed horse."

Lara and I both laughed. I asked, "What did you do?"

"Slapped him, then kicked him out of my house." Lara folded her hands in her lap as Lily Maeve yanked on her toes.

"And what did he do?"

"Married that silly old cafe girl and had himself some kids."

Lara's story quieted the storm twisting through me, but I can't say I really felt better, just settled.

Lara reached up and patted my leg. "You'll never lose Mary altogether. In a while, she'll get lonely for you. The two of you will think back on all the things you used to do. By that time, you'll have found yourself a new friend."

"Who was your new friend?"

Lara leaned back to think on it. "You ever met Jeffery Journiette's wife, MayVelle?"

"Sure enough. She's part of the Bible study that meets at the library."

"She and I could have passed for twins under a long-ago moon."

"What happened?"

Lara leaned back to look me in the eye. "Let's just say you weren't the only one who didn't take kindly to the idea of me courting your papa."

"She stopped being your friend on account of that?"

When Mama left, she didn't see fit to divorce Papa first, so I had my mind set on the idea that Mama would come back and we'd all be a family again. Then Lara stepped in and ruined my whole crazy dream. Back then, Lara was the last person I wanted to be friends with, but I never thought on how it changed her own friendships.

"MayVelle takes to her commandments straight and true. In her way of thinking, I coveted another woman's husband."

And didn't I know the truth of that reaction. I saw Lara as an adulteress until the day she married Papa, maybe even longer. I didn't think kindly on diving into all those old prickly feelings, so

I jumped to a whole other idea that'd been knocking around in the back of my head. I gave Lara a nudge. "You never told me you went to college."

Smiling, she said, "I think my mother sent me to find myself a nice northern boy to marry."

"Well, Papa's from Norway. That should be northern enough for her."

Lara burst out laughing. "Ain't that the truth."

"What did you study in college?"

"History. Philosophy. Literature. I couldn't decide on any one thing I wanted to learn about. In the end, I got a teaching degree."

"You have a degree in teaching?"

"Don't act like that's a miracle, Nissa."

"Hardly. I just never thought of you as a teacher."

Lara sighed. "I came home thinking I'd find myself a teaching job near home, but then my father got sick, and before I knew it, I had a job helping my uncle so I could stay near my parents." Shaking her head, she added, "And they ended up moving back north."

Lara's uncle was the dentist who had an office in the back of his house. I'd met her parents only once. They came to the wedding all jittery and smiling. They'd been promising to come see Lily Maeve for months, but Mr. Ross was poor in health again. Traveling wore him down something awful.

Lara fell silent. Slapping her thigh, she said, "With the new job, I can save up enough to go visit them and show off their grandbaby." Lara scooped up Lily Maeve and tickled her until she squealed.

Feeling guilty for turning Lara on to things that probably

made her feel as soul tired as I did, I asked, "So what made you decide to apply for the job?"

"Your papa said the truth's the truth whether it comes from a child or a tree. Denying it only makes you foolish."

I knew it wasn't the right time to tell her Mama was the one who told Papa the same said thing, so I just kept quiet.

"Besides, with a job at the post office, I can keep Lily Maeve with me. I don't know if I could stay away from my girl for a whole half a day." She kissed Lily Maeve all about the face. Lily giggled and squirmed.

Guilt flared up inside me. April would have to do just that thanks to my suggesting Lara should take Chessie's old job.

"That'll be good," I muttered.

"And howdy." Lara raspberried Lily's tummy.

Watching them laughing and carrying on, I couldn't help but feel a spark of happiness inside me, but it didn't have a chance to spread and warm me up inside until that Saturday at the wedding I'd been waiting half a lifetime to attend.

Mama did herself proud. Not one to cut flowers for a happy occasion, she had the whole house decked out with potted flowers, each pot painted with images of Ira and Rinnie Lee in their life together—planting a garden, playing with their children, sitting out on the porch of the Gator with their friends. The whole effect was like walking into a forest of the future.

Rinnie Lee and Ira stood before Pastor Price, exchanging their vows like they spoke straight to God, all whispers and "amen"s. And when they said "I do," Mr. and Mrs. Villeneuve held out the broom for them to jump, then Otis Dupree signaled the band with a whistling blow on his harmonica.

We scuffed the dance floor Ira built in his front yard near

down to sawdust. With the sizzling beat of the music and the twisting turning of the dancing, folks spread happiness all over the place. You could almost drink it in straight from the air like rain.

Since Carolivia and I didn't take to dancing with foot-stomping boys, we cut our own path across the dance floor. She showed me a step or two, then I returned the favor, knowing all along I'd learned every move from Mama.

As a child I used to sit on the end of her bed and watch her take flight on the music drifting in from the hotel down the street. I tried to dance like she did, but mostly I bruised her toes. Mama said dancing doesn't abide by too much thinking. She told me to let my soul listen in. When the music sunk soul deep, I'd feel the beat of it in my blood, and then I'd have to dance— there'd be no stopping me. That kind of dancing doesn't allow much room for silly things like thoughts, so I just let the music drift in.

Then Mama showed up, all glowing. That woman breathes music like air and makes dancing look as natural as combing your hair.

"I've been watching you, girl." She kept right on riding the beat as she spoke.

"And?"

"You get any better with those two feet and I'm going to have to move on. I don't take kindly to competition." She smiled.

"Go on." I waved the idea away. Mama could pull a crowd into an awed stare with her dancing.

"You calling me a liar?"

The mere idea that I could dance as well as Mama filled me with enough happiness to carry me straight through till Christmas. "Thank you, Mama."

"You've found your own, girl. That's got nothing to do with me."

"And if you believe that, you are a liar."

We laughed, then lost ourselves in the beat.

Thinking back on that night, I see how I may have lost my friendship with Mary and a clear idea of just what I should do with the libraries, but I finally realized how much freedom I'd gained. I could dance without worrying how other people saw me. Lara and I could talk as friends. And whatever choice I made about the libraries, I had the strength to follow it through to the end.

Time and Changes

F olks around town didn't give me much time to decide on any grand new changes for the libraries. Ira gave me a grand tour of the new cannery that left me wondering who'd have the time or energy to even check books out of the library, let alone read them.

One room had a big old metal contraption that reminded me of a combine. That thing washed, skinned, and chopped all of the sweet potatoes. On one end folks had to stand on either side of a moving belt to make sure no rotten potatoes or rocks got in. Along the way folks had to make sure nothing jammed up. At the other end folks kept the potatoes moving along and plucked out any that had hidden rot. I had to imagine all this as Ira told me about each stage. In my head I heard the mind-numbing churn of the machine and saw all those folks, moving like robots to keep up.

In the center of the place sat the cookery—a room full of tin pots the size of most folks' kitchens with temperature gauges and funny little valves. The place probably felt hotter than a boiler room and stank worse than a silo full of manure.

On the canning side folks had to make sure the potatoes went into the cans and filled them up good with just the right amount of sugary water, that the seals had been made, and that no cans had been crumbled in the machinery. The mention of crumbled cans made my hands ache over the thought of crushed fingers.

After the canning came more cooking. Ira said they had to bake out all the germs. Then they slapped labels on and sent the cans along to be boxed up. Folks had to take cans off the belts as fast as they came and drop them into boxes to be shipped. Once a box filled, somebody had to carry it out to the warehouse for storage until the trucks came to haul it off for delivery. The whole place kept in constant motion like some crazed kind of clock. I prayed I'd never have to work there in all my life.

"Want to see the best part?" Ira asked, clapping his hands back together.

"Sure."

Taking me back to the first room, he walked up to this hose that looked like an anaconda long enough to strangle a whale. It reached clear to the other side of that barn long room. Or so Ira told me.

"They've got to keep the place real clean, so nothing dirty gets in the cans," Ira said, taking the hose.

"Uh-huh." I backed up, fearing Ira might see me as an unclean thing.

"There's a compressor pushing the water." He pointed to some engine. "It puts out enough pressure to wash the dirt from the inside of a rock."

Just as he went to show me how that mammoth thing worked, Otis Dupree, Ira's brother Leo, Mr. Garver, and a few other fellas came in. "Playing with the white man's toys again are you, Ira?"

"I'll show you playing." Ira turned and set that hose on those men. It spun them around, knocked them to the ground, and sent them rolling inside a tornado of water.

I squealed to see the show. Ira let up the water and laughed himself silly. The others stumbled to their feet, threatening to skin Ira's hide. Ira wiggled the hose to show folks just what'd happen if they tried such a thing. Those men slogged out of there grumbling and soaked.

Seeing all the water on the floor made me realize just why they'd need a whole sewer system to keep that place in water. "That thing's a weapon."

"Naw." Ira shook his head. "Nobody'll use it on anybody. They've got to hose down the machines at night and the walls and the floors. And after a day's work no one's going to have the strength to think of joking around."

"True enough."

"Now you know what those Yankees have put into your town."

"Thank you, Ira."

And that wasn't all those Yankees had in mind to put into our town. Many of the Northerners decided it was high time for them to donate to the library. For near to a month a different person walked in almost every day with an armload of books, plopping them down, chatting about how they'd come by each one as I went about cataloging them.

One such lady who had an eye made of glass, brought in a stack of children's books. She looked like she might dump the lot of them on the rug when she came in the door. The stack nearly came up to her nose. I still can't see how she made it all the way to the library without dropping a book.

Setting her pile down on a table she put her hands over the books as if to protect them from falling debris. "I'm Mrs. Hazelton. My husband's the night shift foreman over at the cannery." She smiled, but her eyes didn't give me any sign of happiness. One stared at nothing with the blind look of polished glass. The other looked tired, weak, even sad.

"Nissa Bergen." I gave her my hand. Shaking hers, I realized she'd started to tremble, or maybe she had been all along. I figured all that carrying must've worn her out.

Then she started rubbing the edges of a book like someone handles the clothing of a loved one once they're gone. When Mama left town, my Grandma Dee came to stay with us. One night I found her folding up Mama's clothes, looking as if touching the things she wore felt like touching Mama. Seeing *Winnie-the-Pooh* poking out of the stack and catching a glimpse of *The Wizard of Oz,* I realized, Mrs. Hazelton was trying to reach a child through those books.

"Thought you might like some children's books." She forced another smile, but her eyes looked ready to cry, even the glass one.

I nodded. "Kids in town love to read." Part of me wanted to let her know I could see her longing and her loss, but I didn't know how.

"Maybe you could let them know these books belonged to my Willard." She held a book in both hands. "He could read the cover off a book."

My mind flashed on my baby brother, Benjamin. He, like Lily, the sister he'd never know, felt books were best read with the mouth. Death took him before he really developed a taste for the written word, but I couldn't help wondering if he would've been a reader like his papa had he grown.

"Do you want to write something in the cover?"

"Can I?"

"Sure enough." I nodded, offering her a pen. "I've got an inkwell and blotter right here. You can use my desk."

"Oh." She blushed. "Thank you."

I helped her bring the books over to the desk, and she started writing, pressing the blotter down like she patted raw skin after an injury. The deliberateness of it all only made me sad, so I busied myself with shelving other newly donated books. An occasional cough, floor moan, or paper rustle drifted through the stacks as other folks searched for books or read in a side chair.

I came back to the desk for another stack of books. Mrs. Hazelton looked up at me. "Do you run this place by yourself?"

"Carolivia Simpson used to help out, but she turned to canning sweet potatoes when the factory went into full swing." The cannery gave as well as it received. The library filled with the scent of roasting sweet potatoes each day. I had a feeling I'd lose my taste for them right quick.

She nodded, biting her lip. "My husband doesn't believe in women working, but I could volunteer. I'd enjoy it."

If Papa ever tried to tell Mama what she couldn't do, she'd go right out and do that very thing just to prove he hadn't the right. That kind of behavior led me to pity any woman who let her husband twist her life in the direction he wanted it to go. But I smiled, then said, "If you'd like. I could use the company. Truth is, not many folks come in during the week, what with the factory and all."

"Oh, that's fine. I'd appreciate the company myself." She kind of laughed. It sounded all sharp, like breaking glass. "I don't know anyone in town."

Having moved north to live with Mama awhile back, I knew what it was to leave your home and plop down in a place that seemed as strange and far away as Mars itself. "Then it's a deal. Come in when you can."

"Grand." She stood up and shook my hand. Placing her other one on the stack of Willard's books, she said, "Do you mind saving these for me to shelve? I can come back tomorrow."

"Sure thing."

"Thank you, Miss Bergen. Have a good day now." She bowed her head, then went straight out. I still hadn't gotten used to how the Northerners called me Miss Bergen, like they'd taken up a conversation with someone their age.

"Bye," I said as she closed the door.

I set Willard's books aside, then went back to shelving. Long about the time the factory whistle blew for the noon break, Carolivia came storming in through the west side, saying, "Nissa, I've got to renew this here book again." She handed me *Treasure Island*.

"All right." I headed to the desk. "You want to read it a second time?"

"Second time?" She laughed. "I haven't made it through once. Who's had time? First, there was the wedding. Rinnie Lee's dress to sew, the food to make, the house to fix up. Now that I'm canning I can only read on my breaks. By the time that whistle blows, I'm near about ready to hibernate with the bears, I'm so tired."

"I wish I had a job for you here."

"Nissa Bergen, the Harper Crusader." She shook her head. "Don't worry about me, girl. I'm making myself some sweet money. Come schooltime, I'll go home just weighed down with the stuff. We might even be able afford a new icebox."

"That'd be nice."

"That'd mean not having to go the store for fresh every day." She tapped the book. "Renew this here book for me. I've got to have some time to eat before I go back."

As I did just that, I thought on Carolivia sitting out in front of the cannery where Ira had put all the picnic tables he'd built, a sandwich in one hand, a book in the other. Handing the book back, I said, "Do a lot of folks read during break?"

She shrugged. "Can't say. I don't pay attention. I'm reading."

"I see."

"And you'll see me soon enough. Have a good day, Nissa." She ran back out.

I followed her out the door with my eyes. As I turned back, I saw Mrs. Fisher, one of Mrs. Minkie's friends, staring at me from the other end of an aisle of books, looking like I'd let one of the devil's own children into the library. To keep myself from returning fire, I just set right to work.

Shelving books from the wheeled cart Ira made set me to thinking. Not a week earlier Mama had been shouting historical facts down from on top of the shelves. She told me some woman from Maryland named Mary Titcomb had built herself a wagon for books. She took that thing here and there for folks who couldn't get to the library. Nothing said I couldn't have just such a wagon to bring books over to the factory at lunchtime so folks could have something to read. I decided on doing just that.

Right after closing I headed over to Mr. Thurston's shop. The place looked straight out of Chicago, with its polished floors, fancy rugs, and regular old department store displays—a dinning room set up with china, candlesticks, and fresh flowers. I half expected to find a butler waltzing up the aisle with a silver tray, the place looked so fancy. Parlor, study, kitchen, and bedroom setups filled the rest of the place. Mr. Thurston showed off the furniture to his customers like some city slick trying to sell a fancy car with all the newest gadgets.

I hurried to the back to keep from laughing at him. Mama had her elbows into sanding an old wardrobe. I peeked into the back shop to see if I could find Ira.

"What you hunting for, Nissa?" Mama stood up and blew her hair out of her face. I loved how it curled up when the humidity got in between the strands.

"Ira."

"He's making a delivery for some Hazelton fella who bought a new bed."

"I met his wife today. She donated all of her son's books. I think he died."

Mama closed her eyes for a moment. How could I have been so heart cold? She fluttered her lids like she had sawdust in them, letting tears fall. "Can't see giving such things away myself."

Mama still had some of Benjamin's clothes. She kept them in a dresser drawer with little cedar hearts to keep away the moths.

"I suppose she wants other kids to enjoy them." I touched the smooth sanded surface. "She's coming back tomorrow to put them on the shelves. She's going to volunteer every now and again."

"Maybe I should stop over and say how do."

"That'd be nice."

"And what did you want with Ira?" Mama started sanding again.

"A wagon for carrying books to the factory."

Mama stood up, her brow furrowed. "You want to cart books to the cannery? Why?"

"Not too many folks have been stopping into the library lately. I thought I could bring the books to them during lunch break."

Mama slapped the door. "Like Mary Titcomb!"

"That's right."

"Darn if your papa wasn't right to be reading all them books all the time." She shook her head. "Just think where I'd be if I had started reading a lot earlier."

"The moon, I'm sure."

Mama sanded my nose. "You're a little sharp one, aren't you?"

I laughed.

"What do you need Ira for?" Mama stared at me like I'd forgotten something as simple as my own name. And I sure enough did.

"Oh." Straightening up as I would to ask a question in church, I said, "Mama, do you think you could make me a book wagon?"

"Not on your skinny little life."

"Mama?"

"But I'd be proud to show you how."

"That'd be dandy."

"See you after supper." Mama waved with her sandpaper.

"See you then."

Over dinner, Papa took to the idea of a book wagon and insisted on helping. Lara cleared the dishes. Papa and I sat on the

front porch waiting on Mama. She showed up with the old truck
we shared with the Carrolls.

"Evening, Ivar," Mama said, jumping out of the truck.

Papa said his evening with a smile. Even after three years, I
still felt a tiny twinge a hope for the old days whenever I saw
Mama and Papa together.

Mama yanked down the tailgate, revealing the bookshelf
backs yanked from two old-fashioned secretary desks, a beat-up
rusty bicycle, wagon wheels, thick curtain rods, and what looked
like the baseboard of a broken child's bed. It felt like staring into
a mobile version of the old keeping room Lara had turned into a
bedroom.

Slapping her hands together, Mama said, "Let's get started."

Dragging all our materials onto the porch, we Bergens
(Mama by past association) jumped right in. The curtain rods
became guide poles for the bike, the bed base a wagon bed, the
desks—back-to-back—shelves with doors that locked. Rigging
up a tongue from an old wagon I had as a kid to the bike, we
made ourselves a right fine bookmobile. Papa and I dropped
onto the swing in front of our new creation. Mama pulled herself
up on the railing to lean against a post. Lara made her one and
only appearance by switching on the porch light before saying
good night.

We all called back together, "'Night."

That chorus gave me a chill—the family ring of it squeezing
my heart. Mama gave me a know-how-you-feel smile and Papa
squeezed my hand. We all felt it.

"We did ourselves proud," Mama announced.

"Sure did," Papa added.

I felt like saying something about how we could've always

done things together like this, but that'd be wishing Lily Maeve away and ignoring the fact that yesterdays never returned for a second performance like the play folks at the theater where Mama worked. So I just nodded my head, saying, "Uh-huh," knowing a girl's got to be happy with the family that time and changes have left her with.

The Changing of the Guard

he next morning Mama took me to the Harper Hotel for corn bread flapjacks with brown sugar syrup. Mama didn't get along well with the hotel owner, Mr. Cassell, on account of the fact that he didn't take kindly to her voting for herself for mayor when he was the chairman of the election years back. But no one in town made better corn bread pancakes than Helen Borland, the hotel cook. Mama wanted to celebrate my new bookmobile, so we went in and set ourselves down.

Like always, the waitress, Missy LaFavor's sister Vera, took longer than a coon takes to wash its supper just to get to our table. Mr. Cassell put on the brakes when Mama walked in the door—all 'cause she said she hadn't met a man yet who gave a tinker's dam what happened in Harper as long as the Negroes stayed in their place and the women stayed pregnant. That was Mama's reason for voting for herself for mayor some six years earlier. From what we heard in the hotel that morning, I could tell not much had changed since then.

Vera didn't need to take our order—we only ever came there for corn bread flapjacks. But for the time it took her to write our order down, you'd think she'd chiseled it in stone. I didn't pay her any mind as she repeated herself and asked silly things like, "Do you want syrup with that?"

I had my mind set on pretending to read the chalkboard menu while I listened to a group of fellas at another table talking about the cannery. I'd heard tell that a whole mess of single fellas had moved into the hotel from their family farms and such to work in the cannery. A fella with one eyebrow running across his forehead said, "They got them working right alongside us."

"They better not get equal wages, I'm telling you," another answered back. I think it was Winston Caveat's brother, Martin.

"No darkies going to be stealing my wages," Charlie Fisher insisted. He had the same sense of friendliness as his mama.

My mama tapped the table with her butter knife. "Don't let fool talk fill your head. You'll go silly."

"Did you—"

Mama cut me off. "I heard it this morning, yesterday, and thirty years before that. Those boys learned from their daddies, who picked it up from their daddies, and on down the plantation road."

"Them Northerners don't seem to think that way. They hired blacks and whites."

"And probably pay the blacks half as much as the whites." Mama turned her empty juice glass upside down. "Don't go finding saints among the Yampells and their crowd. They're here because they can pay folks half as much and buy raw goods cheaper down here."

"Really?"

"They hire blacks because it saves them money, not because it's the right thing to do."

"Makes a body want to spit."

"Right in their eye, after a long drink of turpentine."

"That's right."

I almost didn't feel like eating our hard-earned breakfast, but a corn bread flapjack soaked in brown sugar syrup is mighty hard to pass up.

After we left the hotel Mama helped me load up the bookmobile before she headed to work. Once I got Mrs. Hazelton familiar with the libraries and such, I headed out with my bookmobile. Even though the cannery only stood a field away from the library, I headed out good and early because I knew pedaling a wagonload of books through tall grass would be as slow going as a wagon train headed west. In fact I imagined wagon tracks leading through the grass. I figured I might just wear those tracks into that field after a couple hundred trips to the cannery and back. Would I still be pedaling that wagon cross-country in a few years? When I looked as old and tired as the Minkies? Felt kind of odd to think such a thing might be so—comfortable in the way you feel when you think on sleeping in a familiar bed and scary like the thought you might live your whole life in the same place without ever knowing a taste of the world.

I rolled right up to a side door around noon. The sheer clatter of the place made my teeth ache. That close in, the noon whistle near about blew my ears clean off my head. As the doors flung open and people poured out for fresh air, water, and a good meal, I shouted, "Care for a book?"

Some folks walked right on by without so much as a look in my direction. Others gave me a glare like I was trying to sell them something. Then I got my first customer, none other than Peter Roubidoux, looking all sweaty and smelling worse. "You got my *Treasure Island,* Nissa?"

"It's checked out, Peter." He'd probably knock out what was left of my hearing if he knew who had it. "How about *Swallows and Amazons?* That's an adventure story."

"All right." Peter licked his lips. They looked dry. "I'll take that."

He took the book, then walked off into the shade. A few other folks walked up before moseying off to the picnic tables under the trees. Watching the tables fill up, I realized only white people sat there. I knew better than to ask anybody about it. When the door stayed closed, I went around back. I could see the last of the black folks heading across the tracks to Rinnie Lee's for lunch. Ira had built all those tables, but he couldn't even sit at them. The white folks of Harper might be steaming over working next to black folks, but the devil still ran the show.

I knew I couldn't get the wagon over the hill the tracks sat on. Pulling the wagon the long way around would take me a lot longer than those folks had for lunch, so I promised myself I'd bring the wagon round to Rinnie Lee's the next day. I kept my promise too.

Mr. Dupree stayed clear, but some folks at the Crocked Gator did check out books from my bookmobile. Rinnie Lee came outside with lunch platters in each hand. Setting them down, she turned to go back inside and caught sight of me. "Nissa, what is that?"

"A bookmobile. I'm bringing books to folks."

"Ain't that the handiest thing." She shook her head in surprise. "That's worth a plate of jambalaya, indeed." Only a tongueless fool would turn down a plate of Rinnie Lee's jambalaya. That stuff's so good, your tummy talks about it for hours.

Stepping up to get my lunch, I said, "Mama and Papa and I made it."

"And you did some fine work too."

"Yes, ma'am."

And that's how my weeks went for a while. On Mondays I took the wagon to the picnic tables. On Tuesdays I pulled it all the way out to the Gator. Truth be told, I brought it home at night, then took it in to the Gator on my way in to work. The rest of the week, I kept to the library, hoping I'd find a way to do all these things and still get my schoolwork done come fall. And, of course, my library still stood divided. But as the weeks passed, it wasn't the only division in town that pulled at people's nerves.

In late July a group of folks started gathering in the library on Thursday nights after supper. I kept the place open and had my meal at the desk on account of the fact that Mrs. Hazelton asked me special could they hold their meeting at the library.

Seeing all the folks who gathered and hearing them talking about how they missed things up North, I soon realized why they needed the library. Mr. Cassell probably wouldn't let them use the hotel. And the veterans' hall gave them the "shivers," as one woman put it. She stood not two feet in front of me and said, "All those photographs of Confederates. How can they honor those men?"

"Don't they know they lost?" asked a man, fanning himself with his hat.

I chomped down on my ham sandwich to keep from yelling,

"Lost? What difference does that make? Plenty of Confederate soldiers lost a lot more than any battle—their lives, their limbs, their homes, their families. And I'm not talking about any slaveholding officer. I'm talking about the men on their feet, fighting for their lives and the right to run their own country."

Besides, Thomas Jefferson backed a war that gave him the freedom to elect his own officials and keep slaves. You can't tell me the Revolutionary War was all that different from the Civil War from the Southern side of things. Don't get me wrong, slavery's an evil thing that chars the soul from the inside, but it was the same said thing back in 1776 too.

My mind still spun from the idea that Confederate soldiers were unfit to even look at. Then those folks settled in around the table. A man with a fancy blue tie knocked on the table, saying, "I'd like to call this meeting of the Harper Improvement Society to order."

You could've rung my head like a bell, the way his words just emptied it right out. The whole idea seemed so crooked wrong that it couldn't be true. I sat there and listened as they talked about better plumbing, better schools, a restaurant fit for proper folks with "mild palettes"—as the lady with the Confederate shivers called them—and improved roads. Each idea seemed more awful than the last. I couldn't believe a one of them, so they just drifted into my mind and didn't settle anywhere. And those Yankees never even once looked my way or paid any mind to me at all. Only Mrs. Hazelton bid me good night. I waved to her in a haze.

Closing up, I wandered home like a soldier rattled by the explosion of shells. I stood on the front porch for the longest time trying to decide if I'd been trapped in a dream. Papa came outside as the bugs started to swarm the light.

"You all right, Nissa?"

"They've formed a group to change Harper."

"Who?"

"The Yankees."

Papa squinted at me. "Sit down here and tell me what you mean." He led me to a swing, and I let all those crazy plans of theirs spill right out of my head.

Papa sat back and sighed. Thinking on it a moment, he said, "Can't see that their ideas are altogether wrong."

"They want to replace Mrs. Owens because she can't see clearly."

Papa's eyes grew wide. "That's wrong. But we're going to need a new school, Nissa. Those folks brought children with them. There's no room in that old place. We should hire a new teacher and divide the school into smaller grade groups."

"You've got ideas, Papa. Everybody does. Why are they doing all the talking?"

"Now, there's the real problem." Papa scratched his head. "Did you say they're meeting there next Thursday?"

"Yes, sir."

"Well, I'd keep this close to heart. We'll get a group together to join our new neighbors next week." Papa nodded, his eyes distant with the plan forming in his mind.

Leave it to Papa to respond with a cool, reasoned plan. I gladly played the role of messenger—slipping letters into books as folks checked them out of the library or the bookmobile, talking to folks who stopped in at the back of Thurston's shop to enlist Mama or Ira in a repair job—all the while stressing how we wanted to surprise those Yankees and stop their carpetbagging takeover. The boys down in Baton Rogue might be falling to pieces without the Kingfish to guide them, but we weren't about to let those Yankees take us on no hayride.

Lara's job as postmistress turned out to be real handy for our cause. Papa figured the library would be full to the rafters by the time the Harper Improvement Society showed up. And indeed you had to make room to breathe in there by the time the day shift at the cannery ended. The doors hung open, the windows had been pushed up, yet folks still kept to their sides of the library like invisible bars blocked their way. Harper could certainly do with some changes, but everyone had a right to a say in what those changes would be for sure.

When the Northerners started coming in, they looked like they'd been arrested and dragged off to jail, the way they slinked along the walls. Mrs. Hazelton asked me, "Did you have another meeting scheduled, Nissa?"

"No, ma'am. We're here for your meeting."

"Excuse me?" the tie fellow asked, like we'd invited ourselves into his parlor.

"We're here to participate." Chessie Roubidoux stepped right up to that stiff fellow.

"I see."

Then everyone started talking at once, shouting ideas about this, anger over that. The place turned into a human beehive that had been woken up from the outside by some honey-loving fool. The tie fella tried to quiet things down, but nobody paid him any mind.

Mama sat on her bookshelf perch, eyeing the ruckus, smiling away like a kid watching a litter full of puppies trying to feed from the same bowl. Finally, she threw back her head and yelled, "Huey Long loved black folks!"

Everyone froze like she'd said God hated humans. Mama spoke loud but didn't shout, saying, "We should elect ourselves a chairman."

Mr. Cassell shouted, "We know who you'd vote for."

The mayor stepped up like he expected to be picked right off.

"Ivar Bergen," Mama yelled. "A man with a head that could stay level on a sinking ship."

"He put up with you," someone whispered, not too quietly.

The mayor laughed at the joke, waiting for things to turn his way.

Other folks chuckled, but Eliah Roubidoux said, "I'll vote for Ivar Bergen."

"Me too," Papa's boss, Mr. Hess, chimed in. And that started an avalanche of votes from both branches of the library. The mayor just sort of faded into the crowd.

The tie fella tried to be heard, but it didn't do him any good. Mama whistled loud enough to make Otis Dupree smile. "This fella down here wants to talk."

"Yes, well, I'm Thomas Yampell."

"The Sweet Potato King!" Mama shouted. Everyone laughed and cheered. Well, the hometown Harper folks did anyway. I believe I even saw a few of the newcomers blush.

"Yes, well," Mr. Yampell looked embarrassed enough to squeeze down into one of his cans. "I'd like to know, are you the man who works for the newspaper?" He looked at Papa.

"That's right." Papa nodded.

"You've done fliers for us, haven't you?"

"That's right."

"My manager, Marshall Carpenter, says you're a good man.

I'll cast my vote for you." Once Mr. Yampell cast his vote for Papa, a tide of northern votes rolled in.

"It's a landslide!" Mama announced, throwing her hands in the air.

"Who is this woman?" Mr. Yampell pointed at Mama as if she might be an uninvited stranger or something worse.

Mama swung around to lean down and offer her hand, "Heirah Rae Russell, Mr. Yampell."

"The furniture painter who works for Daniel Thurston?" He squinted like Mama didn't have a right to be there.

"Furniture painter, builder, repairer, set designer, costume designer, waitress, toilet fixer. I've done many things in my life. But most of all, I figure I'm just a person like everybody else."

Folks burst out laughing over that idea. Mama sure wasn't like most any person we all knew, but she made her point. Mr. Yampell had no right wondering what she was doing there. But Mama always said, men didn't like it when women took charge.

"Let Ivar talk!" someone shouted.

Miss Chessie chimed in, asking, "Did she ever?"

Papa stepped forward and said, "We're not here to argue or make fun."

Mama whirled around to face me, whispering, "Nissa, get your papa a chair."

I ran around the shelves to pull a chair up to Papa. He stepped onto it so most folks could see him. "We're here because Harper's a lot bigger this year than it's been as long as most of us home folks can remember. We've got a lot of new faces but not a lot of room. We need new facilities, like schools, churches, plumbing . . ."

As Papa talked, folks nodded like parishioners agreeing with a sermon. He spoke like a politician who valued truth, like I always figured men such as Abraham Lincoln to sound. Thinking of politicians made me wonder after the mayor himself. Like too many of the officials in Louisiana, he'd said one thing and done another. Scanning the crowd, I saw him standing in the corner like some boy sent there by a teacher. He watched Papa with a knowing look. He'd just ended his time as mayor and he knew it. So did I. And that thought made me ready to float with pride. Papa could make good things happen in Harper. And I longed to see them come to pass.

$\mathcal{R}$eaching

$\mathcal{A}$fter the first town meeting our place became as busy as an anthill. Folks took to stopping by at any old time of the day to give Papa suggestions, each one talking up or talking down the ideas of others. Some even came by just to congratulate him. And if they didn't find him at home, they'd walk right on up to the newspaper office. I'd never seen so many folks traipsing up and down those stairs in all my life.

Papa took to it like a fish to a sandy bank. His mind filled clean up with all their ideas and complaints. The whole of it near about sucked the air right out of him, he fretted so. Pacing the halls, he took a problem and started talking it out—the pros and cons balancing invisibly on his outstretched hands. Papa'd always been a capital problem solver, but the things he decided on had never affected a whole town before.

Even at the supper table, he couldn't keep still. He kept shifting the salt and pepper shakers from here to there, like they represented changes in Harper that he had to try on for size. Lara got to the point that she didn't even put them on the table. Papa started moving other things instead—silverware, serving dishes, even the food on his plate—scraping a bit to the left, then to the right.

"Please, Ivar, just eat," Lara said one night. "If you get any thinner, a good wind could blow you away."

"What?" Papa looked lost in his own kitchen. I felt like he might need a little help getting back to his life.

"Hi there." I waved. "I'm Nissa, Nissa Bergen. Ivar Bergen's girl. You know him, the fella who spends his nights reading in his study or playing with his wee girl, Lily Maeve?" I pointed over to Lily, who reached out for me. I gave her my hand and she started to chew on my fingers. Teething makes chewing a desperate need.

Papa just stared at me a minute, then said, "So I've moved out of my house without leaving. Is that what you're telling me?"

Lara and I nodded. Lily just drooled.

"Sorry." Papa shook his head. "There are just so many things need changing, I don't know what to do."

Putting my hand over Papa's, I said, "I'm not long on answers, Papa, but I can tell you it doesn't pay to find them on your own. You're just mapping out ideas for folks. They'll vote on what they want to do themselves."

I couldn't help but feel like I should've had a town meeting before I built the town a set of libraries. Just building something for an entire town without so much as getting their thoughts on the matter seemed as awful as picking out somebody else's wife. Where had I let my head get to when I thought I had the right to just build a library or two? I'd been spitting mad at those Northerners for taking on the troubles of Harper as their very own, and not a year earlier, I'd done the same said thing. What a sorry hypocrite I turned out to be.

Papa patted my hand back, saying, "You've got a good point there, Nissa. It's not my job to change things." He got up and headed out the door. "I'm just offering up the menu. I don't have to cook the food."

Speaking of food, Papa didn't even finish his meal. Lara and I looked at each other and laughed. She said, "He's gone crazy." Leaning into Lily, she warbled her voice, saying, "Your papa's gone craa-zz-eee." That sent the little one to laughing. Lara repeat herself again and again, making that child nearly go blue with laughter.

Lily Maeve chirped and chortled her way to the end of a trill of laughter, then said, clear as a twig snaps on a cold winter's day, "Papa."

Lara and I squealed.

"Ivar!" Lara shouted.

"Papa, come quick!"

Lily found her first word and treated it like a toy, tossing it out again and again. "Papa. Papa."

Lara and I echoed her.

Papa came running. He slid into the room as Lily Maeve shouted, "Papa!"

Crying and laughing, Papa scooped that baby up and hugged her and kissed her and thanked her until she kicked to get down. "She said, 'Papa.'" He watched Lily scoot off into the hall. Kissing Lara, he chased after Lily, saying, "Now say, 'Mama.'"

I couldn't help wondering what word I mastered first. Listening to Lily Maeve tumble her way through sound after sound for months on end, I knew she'd been practicing her words for quite some time now. "Papa" just happened to be the first one she got down pat. Leaving Lara and Papa to the happiness of their baby's first word, I hunted up Mama to ask her about mine.

Knowing she had supper over at the Gator on most nights, I started there. Rinnie Lee licked her teeth, saying, "You looking for your mama?"

"Yeah."

She pointed across the field toward the libraries. "Take a gander at that."

I followed her hand, and sure enough, there sat Mama on the roof of the West Library. Mama had been known to sit on our porch roof to have a look-see at the stars on any given night, but the sun hadn't even set proper yet. And that roof was a clear two stories off the ground and as slanted as a tree growing out of the side of a hill.

"What is she doing?"

Rinnie Lee laughed. "I'm done guessing when it comes to your mama."

"Me too. I better go ask her."

"Take care of yourself now."

"I will."

I had to lie to myself and say the fear filling my veins only made me lighter as I crawled out onto that roof.

"Nissa Marie, you look like a dog trying to walk across ice," Mama said with a crooked smile. "You need help?"

"I'll be all right." My voice cracked.

"Nissa, you spent a summer on my roof up in Chicago and that's thirteen stories off the ground. What's got you so scared now?"

"Your roof wasn't slanted to dump me on the ground."

"I see." Mama bit her lip. "So what brings you to brave this evil roof?"

"I want to know what word I said first."

A laugh escaped Mama's lips. "Why?"

"Lily just said, 'Papa.'" Sitting next to Mama, I turned to face the scarlet sky of dusk.

"Glory be." Mama drummed her feet on the roof in excitement.

I put my hands down to keep steady. "What did I say first?"

Mama leaned over to kiss me on the check, then came back just a little to whisper, "'Mama.'"

"No surprise there."

Mama took a breath, held it in a bit. I figured she'd drawn in a memory and wanted to hold it for a while. Then she said, "Bennie didn't speak for the longest time. We wondered if he ever would. Then, one morning, he held up his glass and said, 'More, peas.'"

Mama laughed, a tear in her eye. "He always said 'peas' for 'please.'"

"Just like that, he started with a sentence?" Seemed almost like Bennie knew he didn't have the time to waste on any one word.

"Uh-huh. My Bennie was a smart boy." Mama cupped her knees and stared at the changing sky.

After a bit she turned to the window I'd come out of, saying, "A building kind of person could raise up that attic roof there." She pointed to the eave. "Put in a nice old door and have a little porch right out here. A place for sitting and watching the sun set."

"You missing your studio back in Chicago?" Mama and I had built her a studio and a fine garden on the roof of her apartment building.

"And howdy." Mama sighed.

"I don't see why you couldn't make yourself a nice porch up here."

Mama turned her head kind of sideways, like she wanted to ask, "Are you sure you're thinking straight?"

"What?"

"You buy this house since I've been gone?"

"No." I'd done it again. This time I'd taken Lara's house to be my own. "But I could ask Lara."

"I should do the asking, thank you ever so much."

Having Mama say that made me remember back to when she returned to Harper to bring me north. For years before she left, Mama had worked to make the house fit for a lovely kind of living—nurturing a garden that made the myth of Eden seem possible, painting murals on the walls that caused the place to grow like a wood and plaster flower, and adding her tiny touches in every room. The source of all her homebound sorcery had to be the keeping room, that jungle of odds and broken ends. Lara came through and near about erased Mama from the whole place, converting the keeping room, planting new things, and bringing in peculiar furniture. At least she let the murals be. Still, when Mama first saw what Lara had done, she hightailed it out of there. I followed her, apologizing for not protecting all the things she'd left behind.

Mama'd stopped, asking me why I thought I should be the one to save her from her own mistakes. Wasn't I the child? She the mother? Half my life I'd tried to help Mama cope with the gossipy cruelty of the folks in Harper when all along she had to find her own way to happiness.

Now I saw just why I took problem solving to heart. When I couldn't solve Mama's problems anymore, I turned to things bigger and more complicated—a crooked sign of maturity, perhaps, but foolish just the same.

"I've really got to learn when to let other people do what they have a mind to do."

"Noticed that problem, did you?" Mama raised her eyebrows.

I felt like saying she'd been the one to teach me to take on problems, but I held my tongue and nodded.

Mama leaned into me. "Don't fret, Nissa. You've got a good soul that reaches out for people. You just have to learn to wait for them to reach back."

Sitting on that roof, watching the sun slide down the sky like an egg slipping across a pan on a crooked stove, I felt Mama reaching out for me. I took her hand to reach right back.

Strength in Prayer

ate summer brought in a fitful breeze that whirled leaves around in funnel clouds, almost like they'd been churned up by all the activity in town. Folks agreed on the need for a new school. They even turned to President Roosevelt for a little help in building the place. He sent money and WPA workers. The Kingfish lovers hated the idea of taking New Deal handouts, but finding out they too could apply for government jobs sweetened up their tempers. In no time at all, the skeleton of a new building stood in front the old schoolhouse. Everyone figured it'd be a crying shame to tear down the only classroom the white folks of Harper had ever known.

And that wasn't the only construction site in town. Lara had given Mama the go-ahead to build herself an attic studio with a nice porch. But she had a condition. I'd be lying if I didn't say her condition gave my head a spin. Lara insisted that Mama show her how to build. Those women, armed with their hammers and nails, tromped out onto that roof together and made themselves a porch. Inside they knocked out walls for windows, polished up the dusty old floor, and built a fine staircase spiraling down into the upstairs hallway.

Watching Lara and Mama have at the walls with their hammers, I had myself a double vision. I could see Mama on the morning she'd decided our dishes didn't suit her anymore. She'd flung them against the wall, thrilled by the thunder and lightning of the shattering glass. Now she thundered her way through wood. Lara taught me how soul deep good it can feel to destroy a little fruit. If you've got enough anger to twist your reason into knots, then have at a watermelon. Smash that sucker into slushy pieces. And if you've got an enemy, real or imagined, start flinging. Lara brought that same kind of energy to knocking out walls. Seeing those ladies hammer away, laughing, shouting, and having a grand old time, I realized just how Papa could fall in love with them both.

Me, I'd been put in charge of finishing touches—casing in the windows, painting the walls, varnishing the floors. I had no complaints, it gave me a chance to just watch my two mamas at work—a delight in itself.

Besides, I had a bookmobile to keep in motion. As I pedaled to the Gator one Tuesday, I saw a group of folks clustered around someone, rushing across the field toward the tracks. The rigid desperation of their movements told me someone had been hurt. Leaving my wagon, I ran for Dr. Swenson. He drove me out to the Gator.

Leo Simmons sat at a table, his bloody hand set out on towels as Rinnie Lee worked to clean out the wounds in his fingers. Folks surrounded the table, their faces drawn with worry. Leo stomped his feet, shouting, "He done it on purpose. On purpose, I tell you!" All of a sudden, he jerked sideways in his seat, yanking back his arm. "Ahh! Careful, woman!"

"I'm doing my best, Leo."

"Let me see." Dr. Swenson swooped in to help out.

Leo glared at him. "Sure my blood ain't too dark for you, Doc?"

"All blood runs red, Leo." The doctor opened his bag.

"Not for Simon Carroll." Leo threw his head back to give a yell as Dr. Swenson tested the fingers to see if they were broken. "He shoved my hand right into that darn blasted machine."

"Why would he do a thing like that?" Dr. Swenson asked.

"Said he didn't like darky sweat on him."

From the mention of Mary's brother Simon, I'd gone cold and stiff inside. A cruel boy from the day the Carrolls moved to town, I'd always feared his evil ways might turn bloody. Standing there, seeing Leo bleed onto the floor I'd often danced on, I couldn't help but fear for Carolivia and all the other black folks working at the cannery. It just showed me that merging the two libraries into one would only bring about bloodshed—and not my own.

"Rinnie Lee." Dr. Swenson turned to her. "Bring me a bowl, a good-size one."

"On my way." She rushed off.

Mr. Garver's younger brother, Eddie, leaned in to say, "We'll fix that Carroll boy, Leo. He'll know he ain't got no right."

"Yeah," Eddie's pal Hector added. "That boy will learn the advantage of dark skin under the cover of night." Hector slammed a fist into his palm.

"Won't know what hit him." Eddie laughed.

"Cut that talk," Ira shushed them.

The prickly grit of the wall startled me into realizing I'd been backing up as they talked. Seeing the tide of anger turn toward violence, I felt like I should run to warn somebody. But who would I tell? What would they do? Go after Hector and Eddie?

Hurt them worse than Simon had hurt Leo? My heart felt like a fish caught at the end of a hook, thrashing to get free from the fear that held it by a thread.

Rinnie Lee returned with a bowl. Dr. Swenson took it and put it under Leo's hand. "I've got to clean this out, Leo. Then I'll stitch it up for you. Keep it clean and it'll heal well." He pulled a bottle of alcohol out of his bag. "Grip something solid. This'll feel like being struck by lightning."

"I'm ready," Leo said, gripping Ira with his good hand.

When the alcohol hit, Leo screamed like someone'd tried to skin him alive. I hit the steps before I could take a breath. Running clean home, I didn't so much as look back. Panting in the garden, I prayed, "Please bring peace to this town, dear God."

The house stood empty. Stepping inside, I felt just as hollow. I couldn't keep any part of me still, not my mind, nor my heart, nor my body. I had a desperate need to feel safe. I ran for the safest place I knew—my papa's arms. Seeing me coming toward him at a full run, he already had his inky hands out and ready for me.

Holding me close, comforting me with a hum, he said, "What is it, Nissa?"

I looked over my shoulder to find Mr. Hess staring at me from the other room. I figured the kind of news I had should be treated like fire. I couldn't just drop it into the air for fear it'd spread until the whole town had been swallowed up in the flames of violence. Pulling away from Papa, I closed the door to his office. I leaned against it and told Papa everything.

He gasped for air like I'd punched him in the stomach. Standing up, he started to pace. "Did Eddie and Hector leave?"

"No. Should I get Sheriff Denton?"

Papa shook his head. "Definitely not. That man has a wicked streak I'd rather not see in action."

"What then, Papa?"

He still hadn't caught his breath yet. "I don't know, Nissa. I'm not sure there's anything we can do but pray."

It certainly would take a miracle to set things to rights. And only God supplied miracles. Papa and I got on our knees right there in his office. When our voices went hoarse, we got up.

Papa said, "I best go talk to Jacob and Patricia."

I couldn't recall the last time Papa had called Mrs. Carroll by her first name. She could be a stern woman, but Papa knew this kind of news would strike deep into the hearts of Mary's parents. They'd raised their kids to be God loving folk.

"Papa." I took his elbow. "Please take me with you. I don't feel right being alone."

"Sure enough, Nissa." He patted my hand and we headed on over to the Carrolls' place.

Papa knocked. Young Jessup came running to the door, all stomping feet and smiles. "How do," he said through the screen.

"Is your mama or papa home?"

Jessup nodded. "Picking cukes."

The Carrolls didn't have a side gate, so we walked through the house to get to their garden. Papa rubbed Jessup's head as he passed. In the kitchen Papa turned to me, saying, "You should find Mary while I talk to her mama and papa."

"Yes, sir."

I turned to do as I'd been told, knowing Mary wouldn't take kindly to the idea. In the front hall I heard Simon's voice, then laughter from above. Knowing he and his brothers had a room upstairs, I headed on up.

Simon stood inside the doorway of the bedroom he shared with Teddy and Anthony, acting out just how he'd shoved Leo's hand into the machinery. "I fixed that darky good."

"He ain't no darky," I said.

They stared at me like I'd broken into their house to steal the family Bible.

"How you figure that, Nissa?" Teddy asked me, standing. His head near about grazed the slanted roof behind him.

"He's a man. Just like your papa. Just like Jesus."

"You're comparing a black man to Jesus?" Simon rushed forward. I took a step back. "If you were Catholic, I'd say you just earned yourself a seat in purgatory. But I suppose being Baptist means you'll just go straight to hell."

"I'd say you'd know more about that than I do, Simon Carroll. I never tried to cripple a man for sweating."

Simon stared down at me, every muscle in his face tight with anger. Teddy stood behind him, with Anthony only a few feet away. That young boy looked as scared as I felt. Would he help me if his brothers attacked?

Taking a step closer, Simon said, "You can just get your darky-loving self right out of this house, Bergen."

His anger filled that hallway like an evil kind of heat. My body said to run, my mind agreed, but my soul said—stand your ground. And by prayer, I did.

"Now that's Christian love for you. I suppose you're the type of fella who thinks that line about turning the other cheek gives you the right to hit somebody twice."

"Get out of here!" Teddy pushed me. I stumbled, one foot slipping off the top step. The gut sweep of a near fall coursed through me as I gripped the railing.

Backing down the stairs, I said, "Oh, yes, you sure are good Catholic boys. Just overflowing with love, hope, and charity, aren't you?"

Simon stomped down the stairs after me, ready for only God knows what. Then he froze with the stricken look of the guilty. Turning, I saw Jacob Carroll standing there like a father who just saw a part of his son die.

"Pa," Simon pleaded.

Without taking his eyes off Simon, Mr. Carroll said, "Ivar, please take Nissa home."

Papa stood on the bottom step, looking like he'd been ready to jump in and stop Simon from doing whatever he had in mind. Reaching out for me, he said, "Come along, Nissa."

As he led me out the door, I could feel his hand shaking on my shoulder. Free and clear of the Carroll house, he drew me close and squeezed me, saying, "Don't go near that boy again."

"Yes, Papa."

That night the weight of all that'd happened made everything seem quiet and still, the way a place feels after someone dies. Mama came over to stay the night. That death silence must have affected her too, because she told us all to bring blankets and pillows into the dead room. The warmth of a family made safety seem as real as the skin on my face. We passed a book of folktales around the room, taking turns reading out loud—all the time knowing we did it to keep our minds off the truth for just one night. Inside me, in a new place, sore with growth, I felt the solid weight of strength holding me up, pushing me forward to face what was sure to come next.

Staying Safe

Ira woke us all the next morning as he called from the back stoop in a low voice, "Bergens, you up?" Dawn hadn't even ended yet. The whole garden looked purple as we approached the back door. The bookmobile sat by the cherry tree.

Ira smiled, "I figured you didn't want this left out in the open."

"How's Leo?" Mama asked, wrapping her arm over my chest.

Ira sighed. "There's a lot of swelling, but I'm not too worried about his hand, if you get my meaning."

"Uh-huh." Mama nodded, her chin touching my shoulder.

Ira looked behind him. "Folks are playing it safe. Keeping to their own today. You'll tell Thurston?"

"Sure enough," Mama answered.

"Stay safe, Ira." Papa opened the door to shake Ira's hand. "Thanks for bringing the books by."

"My pleasure." He nodded, but he didn't smile.

Lara just stood back in the shadows of the hall, clutching Lily Maeve.

All this talk of fear made me glance over to Mr. Beaurigard's house. An awful run-in with the Klan had left him with a stutter and a lifelong fear of being robbed that sent him to burying his belongings in coffee tins in his backyard. All this trouble for sure had him looking back to the night they set his family's house on fire for buying property on Main Street.

"Take care, Ira," Mama called after him.

I whispered, "Be mindful of angels and stay on course." But I felt like that message really applied to folks like Simon Carroll, not good folks like Ira and his kin.

Turning, I said, "I think I should go over and see how Mr. Beaurigard's getting on."

Mama rubbed my back, saying, "That's a mighty fine idea, Nissa. We'll both go." She gave Papa a reassuring look, and from the fear in his eyes, I figured he needed it.

"All right." He nodded, but he didn't seem satisfied that I'd be safe.

"Ivar." Lara sounded panicked. "Do you think it's safe to stay in town?"

Mama didn't wait for Papa's answer. She scooted us out the back door. As we came out into the alley, she went the wrong way and headed for Jefferson Street.

"Where are we going?"

"Nissa." Mama stopped. "Now, there's doing what's right and then there's doing what keeps you alive until tomorrow. Ira came to our back gate for fear of what the Carroll boys would do if they saw him coming to the front door, but there's no one keeping us from respecting Mr. Beaurigard by going to his front door."

"You mean, showing the folks in town we aren't afraid to be seen with black folks?"

"Exactly."

"Lead on, Mama."

Standing on Mr. Beaurigard's front porch, I felt the heat of angry stares on my back, but I didn't turn. Those fools wouldn't get me to show my fear.

For a bit I wondered if we'd be waking Mr. Beaurigard. Then he peeked through his curtains to see who stood on his porch, looking like he expected to see folks ready to do him harm. I knew he hadn't even thought of sleeping the night before.

Opening the door a crack, he said, "Wh-wh-what is it?"

"Just checking in to see how you're doing, Gabriel." Mama smiled.

"F-fine, Miss Heirah. J-just fine." Mr. Beaurigard gripped the door like it held him up. I wished he had a family to gather round him.

"I mean it now, Gabriel. You need any old thing and you call on us." Mama put her hand over his and gave it a squeeze.

Mr. Beaurigard managed a weak smile. "Thank you k-kindly, Miss Heirah. I'll d-do that."

Mama leaned off the porch to look at the narrow passage between his house and the Carroll's. Then she asked Mr. Beaurigard, "How many windows you got facing the Carroll house."

He closed his eyes for a second. "F-f-four or f-five. I p-p-put blankets over them."

"Good man." She patted his hand. "Let us know if you need boards instead."

"God w-willing, it won't c-come to that."

"God's always willing, Gabriel. His children are the stubborn ones."

"Amen."

"Bye now." She smiled.

I didn't know what to say, so I just nodded my head in Mr. Beaurigard's direction.

"Protect yourself now, Miss Nissa."

"You too, Mr. Beaurigard."

As we came back home, Mama and I heard Papa and Lara shouting it out in the upstairs hallway. Lara yelled, "She can't bring that book wagon anywhere. They could hurt her. She should close the library altogether."

Mama and I froze in the front hall. We could've heard their shouts from anywhere in the house, so moving didn't seem worth the trouble.

"It's not a business, Lara. The library's for everyone in town. You can't just open and close it on a whim."

"You want to see her hurt? I heard how she let Carolivia Simpson go over to the other side." How did Lara know that? Panic started settling in.

"You make it sound like spying during a war, Lara." Papa laughed.

Lara stomped her foot. "This is serious, Ivar."

"I know how serious it is, Lara."

Mama put her hands on my shoulders and whispered, "I told Lara. Your secret's still safe." I took a deep breath of relief.

"If you know, then what are you going to do?" Lara asked.

Papa came to the top of the stairs. He saw me and Mama standing at the bottom, looking up. He said to Mama, "What should we do?"

"Live our life like the devil's looking over our shoulder. Keep a prayer on our tongues and our minds on staying strong."

Papa nodded, but he looked weighted down and tired in a soul beaten kind of way.

"Just what is that supposed to mean, Heirah Rae?" Lara pushed past Papa and started coming down the stairs.

I took a step forward to answer her, but Mama grabbed me by the arm to stop me. "It means you can't run when the evil ways of others start shedding blood. You've got to stand your ground."

"Even if it means risking the life of your child?"

Mama's jaw went stiff. "She's not a child anymore, Lara. Take a good look at her."

My emotions started to shiver. I knew I'd cry if I didn't hold them in. Lara stared at me, her eyes wide with fear. I kept my face still.

"True enough," Lara whispered.

Mama took Lara's hand. "Doesn't mean I'm not scared out of my God loving mind."

Lara rushed forward and gave Mama a hug, the desperate squeezing kind. I looked up to Papa. He bobbed his head as if he knew this was the only path for us to take, but he still feared where it might lead.

Lara and Mama turned and pulled me into their hug— kissing my head, holding me close. They whispered to me, asking me to stay safe, telling me they loved me. It's funny how the most awful things can make feel you so loved.

The Battle

*A*round about lunchtime shouts ripped through the quiet afternoon air like cannon fire. We all jumped in our seats, waiting to hear enough to know who started the ruckus. The Carrolls. The shouting came from the Carrolls. By the low boom of the voices, I figured Mr. Carroll volleyed with Simon and probably Teddy.

Everyone in our house knew folks would start to gather in the street, listening in, but we'd been on the wrong side of that kind of spectacle too many times not to respect the Carrolls enough to stay at home. Mama stuck to cleaning the kitchen wall so she could touch up the mural. Lara rewashed the breakfast dishes. Papa tried to play peekaboo with Lily Maeve, but he kept forgetting to take the blanket down from his face. I set to sorting the books in the wagon for the third time.

The shouting continued for so long, I thought my nerves might snap like old piano wire under the hands of an angry tuner. The crack of a slammed screen door echoed over our way. Don't know if I thought Simon might come down the alley, see me out in the back, then act on his thoughts of revenge. But fear just poured through me like cold water, and before I knew it, I'd run inside and all the way up to my room.

Feeling like a fool, I told myself to go back downstairs. I even gripped the knob of my bedroom door, but I couldn't go any farther. The sound of scattering pebbles whirled me around to face the windows. Mary Carroll ran along the garden wall, looking like the devil himself chased her.

Rushing inside, she pressed the window closed, then yanked the drapes shut. Moving to the other window, she did the same.

"What happened, Mary?"

Dropping down on the window seat, she burst into tears. I sat beside her. Drawing her in, I rocked back and forth, saying, "It's all right." What a fool thing to say.

Stammering, her face streaming wet, she said, "Pa said Simon had to apologize. Simon said he'd rather go to hell." She gripped my arm. "Simon said he'd rather live in hell than work next to a black man. He said that."

I tried to imagine what it might be like to have Bennie grow up to say such a thing, but that boy will stay small and pure in my heart forever. "Oh, Mary, I'm so sorry."

"He's going to hell, Nissa. I just know it." She sighed, all jagged and rough. "And Teddy and Gary will be right there along with him."

"Gary?"

Mary nodded. "I saw him shaking Simon's hand last night. Congratulating him liked he'd won a race or something."

In my mind's eye I could see the three of those boys standing in the street, the hate like glue amongst them. Across town Eddie, Hector, and their friends formed the same kind of group.

All those young men gathering together, acting like soldiers preparing for battle, made me want to run for cover.

"What'd your papa do?"

"He said if Simon didn't care to live by God's laws, then he could live in another house. Simon said he'd be glad to and marched right out. Took Teddy with him."

"Your mama must be heartsick."

"She hasn't stopped crying since last night." Mary wiped her face.

"Your papa will look after her."

"What about Simon and Teddy?"

"If they won't listen to your papa, they sure aren't going to listen to the likes of us."

Mary squeezed me so hard, I thought I'd cough. "Oh, Nissa, I'm so scared, I think my heart might stop."

I hugged Mary, wishing I knew what to say, but I just held on tighter.

It sure didn't feel good to have Mary back in my life under such dark circumstances, and nobody felt any too good about knowing that Teddy and Simon had taken to living over at the hotel with the lot of farm boys over there. I had nightmares about them donning their sheets and heading out into the street with pitchforks and torches. Their boots sent up clouds of dust as they marched toward the black part of town, ready to burn everybody out, starting with Ira and Rinnie Lee.

I woke up in a shaky sweat. Mama had taken to sleeping beside me. When terror struck my dreams, she pulled me close and recited an old Scottish poem her mama used to tell her when she was a wee bitty thing. It began, "The bairnies cuddle doon at nict wi' muckle fash an din." I didn't understand a bit of it, but the soothing music in the Scottish words lulled my soul. I fell back asleep in my mama's arms.

Time's like a scrap of metal in your lung when danger hangs over you. Every beat makes you ache. I thought I'd waste away under the worry of it all, but the battle everyone expected didn't come. Were the boys laying low to plan something? Did they think better of violence on both sides? The uncertainty of it all kept everyone on the edge. Mrs. Minkie took to shouting at everybody no matter what they wanted. Lara near about shed her skin anytime Lily Maeve knocked something over as she skirted along tables and chairs, testing out her wobbly legs.

Mama pushed all her fear and worry down through her hands. She touched up the garden mural in the kitchen, adding lilies. Chisel at the ready, she carved the quiet faces of angels into buffets, chairs, and tables, making a heavenly dining room I longed to rest in. She must've found me snoozing in one of those chairs once too often. I came home one day and found just such an angel watching over my bed from the headboard Grandma Dee and Grandpa Jared had given me years back.

Worry aside, I kept working. I even ran my bookmobile route. Folks didn't say much and they checked out fewer books, but the routine of it helped me through each day. On a Monday in mid-August I'd just started back across the field when Carolivia came running out of the back door of the cannery.

"Wait up, Nissa. I need to return this book," she yelled.

I stopped the wagon and got off the bike, saying, "You can return it later." I kept my eyes on the boys standing around the tables, smoking.

"Why?" She pointed at the cart with the book. "You're here now."

My stalling had done harm. The boys'd had time to see Carolivia. They started toward the cart—Teddy, Simon, and Peter Roubidoux. "God help us," I prayed.

Carolivia turned. "What do they want?"

"Just what do you think you're doing, girl?" Simon spoke to Carolivia, but Teddy kept his eyes on me.

Before Carolivia could answer, Peter jumped forward, yanking the book out of her hand. "This is mine! I gave this book to the library!"

Simon loomed over me, making me pant like a darn dog. "We overlooked how you catered to those darkies with your little book wagon and your library's fancy painted back room, but you aren't giving them our books." I hadn't even seen him take the book from Peter, but he walloped me upside the head with the thing.

Flung into the grass, I went down on all fours, my head throbbing, the ground swirling beneath me.

"Get out of here." Simon kicked me.

It felt like he sent a rib right through my back. I heard Carolivia screaming. Knowing Simon could beat me all the way back to the library, I rolled over, scrambled to my feet, then fishtailed it around the book wagon.

He came running after me, and I shoved the cart hard. That wagon came down on him like a stone wall.

Teddy had Carolivia by the hair. Peter hit her like I'd seen farm boys punching at a sack a grain to build up their strength.

Charging like a crazed horse, I took Peter to the ground.

Simon started screaming for Teddy.

As I got up, I saw a swarm of folks crossing that field, black and white. The battle had begun, all over some damned book.

Ira sheltered Carolivia. Mr. Dupree went after Teddy. Mary's brother-in-law, Martin, ran to help Simon. Everyone went after somebody, kicking, biting, and screaming.

April tried to pull me clear of the fight, but I yanked myself free. Running, my side felt like it'd been cut clean open. Going straight for one of the cleaning hoses, I prayed it'd reach. The on valve wouldn't give. Crying, I grabbed the hatchet dangling by the fire alarm. I set off the fire alarm with a solid whack, then used the back side of the hatchet to knock that darn valve full open.

Dragging that hose took all I had, but I let that water rip, blowing men right off their feet. The squeal of a siren didn't turn me away from my job. I hosed those men who'd gone wild with rage. When Sheriff Denton tried to take the hose from me, I turned it on him. Papa's warning about that man made me fear he'd only make matters worse.

Folks tried to come after me, but all that water had turned the field into a mud pit. They slipped, fell, slid. Before long, nobody could stand. Other folks from town had arrived. They started pulling folks out of the fray, quieting them down, leading them off.

As the field started to clear, I saw Mama standing on the other side of the bookmobile looking like she just might rise up into air like an angel herself.

Papa swung around behind me, hugging me, telling me to let go. Seeing Mama's face let peace wash over me. My hands went limp. I fell into Papa's arms and a darkness filled with numbness.

Sainthood

*P*apa's tearstained face looked down at me as my eyes fluttered open. My face felt about as large as a pumpkin—swollen, stiff, and sore enough to make a girl cry. I couldn't breathe without wincing for all the pain in my side.

Papa rubbed my tummy to soothe me.

"Carolivia?"

Papa sniffled. "Doing well. They sent her home."

"Back north?"

Papa nodded.

I felt liked I'd been kicked all over again. My new friend gone, just like that, and I didn't even get to say good-bye. Darn if that didn't just crush my insides. My thoughts turned to Simon, which only made me feel worse.

I feared the answer like a liar fears the truth, but I asked, "Simon?"

"He broke a leg and two ribs."

"No, Papa. I did."

"To defend yourself." Papa gripped my hand as if he thought I might slip away.

"You always told me never to hit another person."

"Nissa, that boy could have killed you." He shuddered.

I'd dumped that wagon over on Simon without so much as a thought. It scared me clear down to the raw center of my soul to think how easy it'd all been. "I could've killed him."

"But God didn't let that happen."

"Mama. I saw her. Is she all right?"

Papa's face got all strange, like he couldn't get any air.

"Papa?"

"Heirah's a little beside herself."

"Where is she?" I called out to her. "Mama?"

Papa put his hand on my chest. "You lie still now, Nissa. I'll tell your mama you're asking for her."

I gripped Papa's hand. "Is she all right?"

"She'll be fine, Nissa. Once she knows you're all right." Mama had faced the death of too many children already—Bennie and the babies who never had the chance to be born.

Papa went to get Mama, but he sent Lara into my room.

I sat up before Lara could stop me. It felt like somebody stabbed me in the side. "Where's Mama?"

Lara sat so close to me, she almost sat on me. Putting her weight on my leg, she said, "You've got a broken rib, Nissa. Too much moving around could send it into your lung."

I didn't care much about breathing right then. "Where is she?" I screamed.

"On the roof of the library." She pulled the covers up to my waist. "We think she's praying."

"On the porch?"

"No." Lara looked off to the side. "On the top of the roof, closer to God up there, I guess."

"Did she say anything?"

"No."

Lara's closer-to-God idea made me see that even Papa had read Mama wrong. Mama wasn't up there fretting after me. She didn't believe heaven hung above us like some celestial island. You got closer to God in your soul, not by climbing higher. I lay back down knowing somehow that Mama was safe. I fell asleep believing it.

I heard whispering when I woke up—a steady, rhythmic stir of voices below me. Slipping out of bed sent a ripple of pain through me, but I ignored it and tiptoed out into the hall. At the top of the stairs I could tell the voices came from the dead room. Panicked, I feared Simon had died. I'd killed a boy. Ended a life.

Bursting into the dead room I found a gathering of folks on their knees, praying under the leadership of Pastor Raymond Price of Revival Baptist. All my kith and kin collected in one room—Mama, Papa, Lara, Ira, Rinnie Lee, Mr. and Mrs. Villeneuve, even most of the Carrolls—Jacob, Patricia, Mary, April, her baby Franklin, Anthony, and little Jessup too. And right there beside Papa knelt Gabriel Beaurigard.

I started to get on my knees, but Pastor Price saw me and came up to put his arm over my shoulder, saying, "This child here is in God's hands. He showed her how to wash those men clean of their anger. While men were led to violence, this child kept her mind on peace."

I'd kept my mind on trying to keep people from killing each

other. And hitting them seemed a damn fool way to go about it. The hose was the only thing I'd ever seen strong enough to take on an entire group.

Folks started saying their "amen"s and "thank the Lord"s, and I felt like a beggar who'd tried to slip into a hotel by stealing a priest's frock.

"Stop, please stop."

Mama stood, her face all glowing like that day in the field. Stepping forward, she said, "My girl ain't one for praises." At my side she turned to face everyone, saying, "Pastor Price said it right. God gave Nissa the strength and the ideas. My girl's a good child." Mama put her hands on my shoulders. They felt hot with love and pride, as if all her emotions had turned to energy and she pumped them right into me. "We'll let her rest."

"Yes, you should bring her back to bed." A voice came from the corner of the room, and I saw Mrs. Agnes Minkie sitting in a chair all teary eyed. Feeling like I'd seen a miracle—Agnes Minkie sitting in my house—I let Mama lead me on to bed. Folks sent me off with "God bless you"s.

Mama tucked me in. Taking her hand, I said, "What were you doing on the roof?"

Mama looked both ways, like she didn't want to let our eyes meet. "Trying not to fly."

I felt laughter bubbling up inside me. "What?"

She gripped my shoulders, pressing in tight, hugging me in the only way she could. "Girl, you filled me with enough pride to send me around the moon." Holding up two fingers, she added, "Twice."

I started bawling.

"I mean it. Hosing those fools down. Sending them into the

mud like so many pigs, every one of them coming up as dirty black as the next. They all looked the same. God creates such amazing pictures for the soul to see." She laughed.

"But I hurt Simon."

"Slowed him down enough to let good sense catch up to him."

"Really?" I held her elbow.

She patted my hand. "He'll mend, Nissa. In body. I'm far more worried about his soul."

"Folks talking about revenge? Fighting again?"

Mama laughed. "No. Everyone's talking about that Nissa Bergen taking down two boys twice her size and hosing down a field full a lunatics. Nissa, you sent the sheriff into the mud."

We giggled, me holding on to my side, Mama bending down, until her tears fell on my face. She wiped them away. "Your grandma's coming. And both of your grandpas, too."

"Grandpa Knute's coming from Minnesota?" I'd never even met him. He only spoke Norwegian. I had no idea what we'd say to each other.

"That's right." Mama kissed my forehead. "They all want to celebrate their little saint." She pulled at my nightgown.

"I'm not a saint, Mama."

"Tell me about it." She rolled her eyes. "And don't you let them have at that nice piece of humble pie you've got stored in this here heart." She rubbed my chest. "But you can't blame them. It isn't every day a granddaughter stops a riot."

"But nothing's really over, Mama." I knew folks that mad didn't let their anger just slide off them like so much water.

"I know." She took a deep breath. "There's a bit of the need to protect their young that's driving them here." Mama spoke the truth. A few years back when my fear of losing Mama drove me into a river even though I didn't know how to swim, Grandma Dee came to Harper to keep me safe.

"People don't really think I did a miracle or something, do they?"

"Not really. They're just all so shocked. The violence. The fact that you did what none of them figure they'd have the strength to do."

Warmth filled me in a way that made me feel afloat. God's love. His way of thanking me for doing what He asked, I guess. And as the warmth faded, tiredness seeped in.

"Tell me bairnies, Mama. Tell me bairnies."

"The bairnies cuddle doon at nict wi' muckle fash an din. . . ."

⊱ Friends, Family, & Fire ⊰

*M*ary came in through my bedroom door as I tried to get dressed the next day. "Don't you know how to knock?" I asked. I didn't like the idea of her seeing me moving around like some half-frozen bear, doing something as simple as putting on a shirt.

She dropped down on my bed, saying, "But, Nissa, you've got to hear what everyone's been saying."

I felt like reminding her of what she'd said under our cherry tree awhile back, but with all that'd happened, I couldn't be that small. "What?"

Helping me put on my shirt, she asked, "How's it feel to have a broken rib?"

"Pray you'll never know."

"Well, I do know that Sheriff Denton tried to have you arrested."

"What?"

"That's right." She hopped in her seat. "He wanted you arrested for assaulting an officer, but the parish sheriff, a fella named Talson, wouldn't hear of it. Mr. Hess and Mr. Cassell called that man in because they didn't like how Denton handled the whole thing. He tried arresting the whole fighting lot of them. Everybody knows we've only got one jail cell. He thought we could lock them in the old livery like a herd of horses."

I couldn't believe the idea of throwing a bunch of muddy, angry men together in some drafty old barn. "You don't say?"

"That's right." Mary looked real serious all of a sudden. "The parish sheriff showed up quick as you please. He fined every adult who raised even a voice for disturbing the peace. Five dollars for the whites. Ten for the blacks. Said they'd started the riot. When someone pointed out that Simon and Teddy and Peter started it all, he said that was sure enough true, but then it was just a fight among some young kids. The black men were the ones to start the riot."

"That's what he said?"

"He really said, 'You boys,' and he pointed at the black men in the room. They held all this over at the veterans' hall."

"What about Simon and them?"

Mary closed her eyes for a second, then said, "Simon's nineteen. He's really an adult, so they had to arrest him for assault."

"I dropped a wagon full of books on him."

"They said it was self-defense." Mary put her hand on my thigh. "And I believe them."

"Thanks," I whispered, still feeling guilty.

"Teddy and Peter are only seventeen and sixteen, so they were given suspended sentences. They've got to mow the cannery lawn, reseed the field—it's a muddy mess." She patted my thigh. "And get this. They've got to mow the library lawn and clean the place from top to bottom for one whole year."

"No?"

"Yup."

"Will Simon go to jail?"

Mary shrugged, bowing her head. "Pa says it'd give him time to turn from his evil ways."

"I'm sorry, Mary."

"Oh, no." Mary shook her head. "It's all right. I think Pa's right."

She smiled at me.

I smiled back.

"Do you know the best part? Besides you being okay."

"What's that?"

"Gary says all that fighting showed him God'll protect a peace loving man."

I nodded, thinking Gary to be more of a coward than a Christian. "That's great."

Real great. Mary would go right back to spending all her time by Gary's side.

I asked, "Is Simon in jail with his broken leg?"

"No, he's under house arrest at our place. They said he can't leave. Can't even go on the porch."

I would've been afraid to sleep in the same house with the boy, but it didn't seem right telling Mary that.

"Pa put him in the attic. He locks the door at night, so Simon won't try to leave."

That'd make me feel a little safer.

Leaning into me, Mary said, "I can't believe all this has happened."

Even though I knew the impossibility of it, I said, "I hope it's the last of it."

"Me too."

Mary and I sat shoulder to shoulder, and it felt heart good.

Lara came in all jittery. "You'll never guess who's coming."

"Your parents!" Mary and I shouted together.

Lara looked like we'd told her what she'd get for Christmas for the next ten years running. "That's right. They're coming to see their new granddaughter receive her award."

I expected her to say, see their new granddaughter talk or maybe even walk, but I had no idea there'd be an award in the mix.

"How so?"

"Oh." Lara covered her mouth in shame. "I wasn't supposed to say." She stomped her foot. "Darn my flapping mouth."

I turned to Mary. "What is she talking about?"

Mary squealed. "Mayor Kinley is going to give you a good citizen award. It was Thomas Yampell's idea, but the whole town committee voted for it."

"You don't say?" I sat there as stunned as if they'd told me I'd have a second head growing out of my ear come spring.

But they spoke the truth. That Saturday, I'd be given an award for good citizenship in the libraries I'd started.

Folks started pouring in for the event. The Rosses came, Mr. Ross looking peaked but happy. They cooed and cuddled with Lily Maeve and kept shaking their heads at me, saying things like, "Such a little thing to do such a big job."

Grandma Dee and Grandpa Jared arrived next. Grandma Dee nearly jumped out of the truck before Grandpa Jared could come to a stop. She had her arms out to hug me, but Mama caught her up in a hug first, saying, "Remember Nissa's rib, Mama."

"Oh." Grandma covered her face with her hands. Then she came to me, kissing me all about the face. "I love you, child. I love you."

"I love you too, Grandma Dee." I kissed her on the check, wishing I could hug her.

"So proud." Grandma Dee had started to cry as Grandpa Jared came around behind her. She took his hand. "We are so proud."

"This is better than seeing one of Heirah's plays," Grandpa Jared shouted, shaking my hand. "Well"—he stole a glance at Mama—"about equal."

"Equal, my eye." Mama spit. "This girl's a hero." She winked at me. "And we need to celebrate!"

That set everyone into motion. We had salt-cured ham, pickled beets, fried okra, sweet potato pie, mashed potatoes, and more corn on the cob than a mess of hogs could eat. We had picnic tables out in the middle of the street. Folks kept coming up with more food to share. As I got myself another cob, I heard Chessie Roubidoux say to Mrs. Linzy, "Next thing you know, they'll be giving her mama a good parenting medal. A hero. That girl is as touched as her mother."

I looked straight at Miss Chessie. She stared right back, her lips in a rare moment of silence. Nothing I could say would change her evil mind, so I just turned and left. As I did, I heard her say, "I'm only here to eat before I go to work. Can you believe they stuck me on swing shift?"

Walking back to my table I saw a man coming toward us, a carpet satchel in his hand. The hat on his head looked like the kind fishermen wore when they went to sea. His shoulders stooped, his beard long, he looked like he'd retired long ago.

Dropping my plate, I walked forward. "Bestafar Knute?" Papa had taught me how to say "grandpa" in Norwegian.

He let go of his satchel and cupped my face in both of his

callous hands, saying something like, "Mitt dyrebar, Nissa." On his tongue my name sounded like music.

I hugged him, devil take my darn rib. He smelled of dust and wood smoke, so much like Papa. And the way the lines under his eyes looked like smiles—he sure was his son's papa.

As I let go, Papa came up and hugged Grandpa Knute, speaking to him in Norwegian. I loved the sound of Papa's language and once again regretted that I'd never learned it.

As Grandpa Knute ate, he kept looking at me, then shaking his head.

"What is it, Papa?"

Papa smiled, rubbing my head. "He says you look like Grandma Nissa."

"Bestemor Nissa." Grandpa Knute nodded.

Even though it hurt, I smiled so wide my lip nearly split open. And that prideful happiness carried me on a cloud right to the library, where practically the whole town gathered to watch me receive my award. I felt as if I'd walked through a field of stinging nettles. My skin burned with embarrassment as I stood up in front of everybody. The award Mayor Kinley handed me was a medallion on a red ribbon. I felt a little like a racehorse receiving its ring of flowers as he put it over my neck. I looked at all those folks, so happy with the thought of being together and safe. Darn if I didn't feel like I could float right up through the roof.

The award given, everyone talked and laughed and congratulated me. With all that racket nobody really noticed the first scream. Then the whole West Harper Library filled with screams of horror. The shriek of an alarm echoed them.

Someone yelled, "It's on fire! The cannery's on fire!"

That set a flood in motion, everyone pushing to get outside.

Some men ran the other way—volunteer firemen off to get the truck.

The flames lashed at the dark night. I prayed someone could get to the cleaning hoses to put that darn fire out as folks ran across the field to go help. I followed. Papa caught me before I got close enough to feel the heat of the flames. "You've done enough, Nissa. Leave it to folks who are fit."

The workers poured out of the factory, dazed, sooty, and coughing. Some held others up.

Someone threw a rock at a window. "To let the smoke out!" he shouted. Others threw rocks or ran in to see if they could help. A howling scream came from the far end.

"It's Chessie!" Mr. Minkie pointed with one hand, covering his upper arm with the other. Chessie Roubidoux thrashed in front of an open window, her hair on fire. Seeing a human on fire is like watching hell open up and swallow a person whole. Someone broke through a door to wrap Chessie in something I figured to be wet.

Just before the fire truck arrived the water from the cleaning hoses started spurting out the windows. The firemen trained another hose on the flames shooting out of the roof. Together, they beat that fire down into a sooty black scar. The injured were taken away, some, like Chessie, rushed to the hospital over in Mercane.

Mama came to me, sooty and coughing but safe. She put her arm over my shoulder, saying, "Fire may be a cleansing way to clear out a dead garden, but only the devil would use it to destroy the unwanted."

She had set fire to the tangled remains of the garden when we moved into our house on Main Street, so she knew the purifying power of fire firsthand. Had some crazed fool thought setting the cannery on fire would push the Northerners out and return Harper to the way it had always been? How could they see past the damning act of murder? I figured Pastor Belmin's soul wept that night, seeing how so little had changed in almost thirty years. I wept with him.

The Right Thing by Degrees

*I*n no time at all the sounds of hammers filled the air like some strange kind of bug. The Yampells didn't see no reason to hold off on rebuilding. As I heard Mr. Yampell say at the post office, "Folks have to work. They've got families to feed."

He walked on out the door with his fancy suit and fedora hat as he pegged himself for a New Dealer bringing jobs and food to the starving folks of the South.

"Don't you just want to send him out in the field to pick rock?" Lara said, leaning on the counter.

"And howdy."

Mrs. Linzy rushed in, practically sweating with worry. "Have you heard after Miss Chessie?" Folks still treated the post office as the news center of town.

Lara stood up straight, taking the responsibility of spreading news like an honor. "Eliah stopped in this morning, saying she wouldn't stay at the hospital. He brought her home."

"She all by herself?"

"No, no. Eliah and Kate are looking after her."

"I best go see her."

Lara did something Chessie Roubidoux would never think of. She came around the counter and took Mrs. Linzy's arm. "Opal, you might want to think on that for a bit."

"Why?"

Lara whispered, knowing she shared private things in a public place. My, how the post office had changed. "The fire took most of her hair and burned her clean down to the shoulder. She's just rock bottom ashamed to be seen. That's why she insisted on coming home."

"Oh, nonsense. She'll want to see me." Mrs. Linzy walked off acting as if Lara had told her Miss Chessie had a run in her stockings and didn't want to show up in church in such a state.

Lara stared off after Mrs. Linzy.

I said, "A friendship like that one should end."

She looked at me. "Do you think it'd give either of them the room to let their hearts breathe?"

"Miracles do happen."

Lara walked behind the counter. "We could use a few around here."

Seeing the two sheriffs drive by, I asked, "They find anything at the cannery?"

Lara shook her head. "I feel like I should put a radio booth over there." She pointed to the corner where Lily Maeve played in her crib. "The news comes in here like rain through a leaky roof. I might as well begin broadcasting."

"Do tell." I leaned in close.

"They found bits and pieces of a box of rags in a storeroom. The whole lot smelled of gasoline."

"No?"

"Afraid so."

The cannery had concrete floors. Only the oil on the machinery burned. The wooden walls and the roof couldn't stop a fire, but saddest of all, the flames had to go through the people first. With the sprinkler system, the cleaning hoses, and the fire department, they got that blaze under control mighty fast. Thinking on the cannery fire filled my mind with visions of what would happen if someone set fire to the libraries. Books burn like oil. There'd be no saving the people inside the libraries. Now I knew for a lifesaving fact that making them into one library would've been a foolhardy thing to do. It surely would've ended lives. How could people be so dead inside that murder seemed like a solution?

Lara forced a smile. "They'll find out who did it. Whoever it was is going to jail."

That fact made me hungry for another. "Thank you, Lara. I'll see you for dinner."

"Okay. You all right?"

Waving without looking back, I said, "Sure enough."

I moved slow, but the walking did me good, kept my muscles working so they didn't rust up on me. At the shop I found Ira watching Mama carve two children holding hands in the headboard of a cradle.

"How do."

Ira turned. "Your mama has got hands that could decorate heaven."

Mama blew sawdust in his face. "Not hardly. You think they'll be needing any of this junk in heaven?" She pointed at the other furniture.

Blinking and wiping his face, Ira laughed. "I suppose not."

"Leo doing well?" I asked.

Ira nodded, but he frowned. "Still mean angry, that boy."

I felt like asking, "Angry enough to set a fire?" But like everyone else, I suspected the hand that set that fire belonged to a white man.

"Did they ever find out who started the fire in the church?"

"What church?" Ira stood up like I'd screamed fire.

Mama yanked on his sleeve. "Belmin's, silly. She's talking about Belmin's."

"Oh." Ira kind of shrank into himself with embarrassment. "Why you always asking about that place?"

"Please, Ira."

"Well, if you've got to know, then the answer's different depending on who you're talking with."

"How so?" As I used a chair to get up on a buffet, Ira came to stand next to me and Mama set back to work.

"See, the fellas who started the fire figured they'd done the whole parish a service and spread the word, but they did it in the funny silent kind of way gossip has of traveling. You know, around sheriffs and stuff."

"So folks knew who did it, but the fire starters were never arrested."

"Uh-huh."

"Who did it?"

Mama straightened out her back to stretch it, saying, "Local Klansmen like Clem Thibodeaux, Albert Minkie, and Harrison Cassell."

"That's right." Ira looked shocked and impressed. "How'd you know that?"

Mama wiggled her fingers. "Their rings. Only three men in town have a ring that they didn't get on their wedding day. Those three. I never figured them for the college type. Besides, I've seen the scars on Minkie's arm."

"Nothing passes your eye unnoticed, Heirah Rae."

I'd seen the ring on Mr. Minkie's finger time and again, but I never did connect it to Mr. Cassell's. And I don't know that I ever noticed Clem Thibodeaux's. I tried not to let my eyes settle on that man. I did recall how Mr. Minkie held his arm at the fire. Did it remind him of what it felt like to get burned? Those three men had killed an entire family.

"But they murdered people."

Ira sighed. "True enough. But folks all saw their deaths as an accident. No one figured anyone was inside the church. The Belmins had a house all ready for them, but they hadn't moved in yet. No one knew that."

The way gossip flew through the parish, they darn well should have. "That doesn't mean those men should get away with murder." And they all owned businesses in town. We bought groceries from Minkie.

"Why do we pay that man money? Buy things in his store?"

Mama put her chisel down. "The Vincentville mercantile is run by a Klansman as well. After that, the next nearest mercantile is thirty miles away, Nissa."

"But Mr. Minkie is a murderer!"

Ira fell silent as Mama asked, "What do you figure we should do? Kill him for it?"

"Send him to jail."

"On what evidence?"

"I hate this town!" I stomped out the back door, but I didn't get far. All that screaming and carrying on had made my side ache.

Mama came out and stood behind me. "We came to Harper for the newspaper job. Papa got the house for as long as he worked for Mr. Hess. We didn't get any money for the house on Wakefield Road. I couldn't live there anymore. I heard Bennie in the wind." I didn't face her, but I could tell Mama had started to cry. That brought tears to my eyes. "So we sold it for less than we owed the bank."

Mama waited a bit, then she went on. "That's why your Papa had to stay. He owed Hess for the house—the banknote that old coot paid off. Leaving meant bringing the law down on us."

"I never knew any of that." I turned around.

Mama cupped my face. "I do know how to keep a secret, Nissa." She smiled, slow and careful, knowing how her words would settle inside me like rocks. Mama had shared so much of her life with me, I often forgot we weren't just best friends. But now I knew she'd left Papa nailed down in Harper—a town that could kill and let the killers own half the businesses.

"You left Papa with all that, but even then you couldn't stay away. This awful place just sucked you back in."

Mama put her head against the side of the building. "For every Chessie Roubidoux, there's a Rinnie Lee. For every Harrison Cassell, there's an Ivar Bergen. And don't you forget the devil's got a great singing voice."

"What?"

"Lucifer started out as an angel, head of the choir, according to the pastor of my girlhood church. Even the evil one himself has good deep down in there somewhere." Mama raised her eyebrows at me. "We all know good folks have their share of evil ways. You can't pack up an entire town and cart if off to hell. You've got to stand your ground and do the right thing."

These words from my mama—the woman who packed a suitcase and walked out.

She stepped forward and covered my mouth, knowing I couldn't let her just say such a thing. "Some of us aren't as strong as others. We've got to leave, build our souls up, then come back ready for the fight."

Mama dropped her hand. I asked, "Living examples of doing right?"

"Trying to anyway." Mama nodded.

"That's why you're back? To show folks how to live a proper life?"

Mama tapped the porch in front of me. "No, I'm leaving that up to the likes of you and your papa. My job's making sure no one takes you away before you're through." Her face looked too still. I felt cold inside.

Mama didn't think herself worthy. A younger me would've hugged her, crying out how much I loved her, until she felt that worth in her heart. But now I knew better. "I'm only trying to do what's right, Mama."

"This I know."

"I'm not a miracle worker."

"No, I leave that up to God. But do you see other folks building libraries or running newspapers?"

"Building furniture."

"Furniture rots, Nissa. Ideas don't."

Stunned into silence, I just stared at Mama.

"You wait and see, Nissa girl. Those ideas'll grow. Give it time." She laughed. "Show folks you learned patience from your papa, not your mama."

Smiling, I said, "Most folks wouldn't print what I've learned from my mama, but they'd benefit by it just the same."

"Come here, girl." Mama wrapped me in her arms without squeezing. I snuggled into her and thanked God for bringing her back into my life.

That night over leftover mashed potatoes and gravy I realized something. Harper probably began as hunting grounds for Indians. One hundred years ago the land on which I lived had been a plantation. Sixty some years ago a town rose up. Thirty years later some of the folks from town burned a church down for opening its pews to whites and blacks alike—killing an entire family. The killers walked free, even running things in town. Now a new generation had tried to burn out the idea of taking the road toward equality. But that fire had been put out. The law hunted for the fire starters. Sure, they did it on account of the money the Northerners brought in, but what brought slaves to this country? What kept them in bondage? Money and power and the human greed for both.

Still, things changed for the better by degrees. Harper now had a library. Blacks and whites worked side by side. They built a new factory together. Like Mama said, you've got to give ideas time to grow. It was a crying shame that things so evil had to take so long to die, but I could hear the funeral music in my head— like a radio playing in a house down the street.

Give it time. The place would grow. Me right along with it.

⊰— Ideas That Grow —⊱

ama knew a lot about growing ideas. She'd taken on learning how to build things. Then Lara latched on to that idea and helped her build a studio. Mama started painting flowers on furniture. Then April and Mary asked her to come over to April's to show them how to transform a stuffy old dresser into something fit for Franklin's room. But best of all, the Rosses and Grandpa Knute took to Mama's idea of moving close to family. Grandma Dee and Grandpa Jared couldn't stay—they still had a farm to tend in Mississippi, but the Rosses rented a nice little house behind the mercantile, and Grandpa Knute took up quarters in our keeping room.

One morning he found me in the kitchen cutting beans for Lara to can. Dropping a dictionary in front of me, he said, "Teach." He touched his chest.

Shocked and giddy, I held up a bean. "Bean."

On cue Grandpa Knute and Lily Maeve said, "Bean."

They both laughed and got a bean in reward. I taught

Grandpa Knute English and he taught me Norwegian. *Uff da,* that was a tough job, for both of us.

And the ideas flowed right through town. Mr. Yampell made a big announcement at the next meeting of the Harper Improvement Society—come the end of October, the new school would be ready for students. Apart from us Bergens, only a handful of folks had gathered for the meeting—the Minkies, the Linzys, the Thibodeaux brothers, Mrs. Owens, Mayor Kinley, Mr. Cassell, the Yampells, Mr. Carpenter, a fella named Potter with his wife and brother, and the Hazeltons. Besides the painful absence of any black folks, it seemed so odd to have Chessie Roubidoux missing from such an event. But then Miss Chessie hadn't so much as looked out a window since she'd moved to her brother Eliah's.

Mr. Yampell expected his announcement to cause a big stir. Instead the small group gathered at the table stared back at him, waiting for his next plan of attack.

Putting his hands flat on the table, he said, "So of course we'll need new teachers."

Papa licked his lips, saying, "Well, with all the new children moving in, it appears that we'll have about two hundred sixty kids or so. The school at the end of Jefferson will not hold over one hundred kids."

"Jefferson?" Mr. Cassell barked, waving his ruby-ringed hand around. "What's that swamp school got to do with us?"

I felt like yanking that ring off his finger and shoving it down his throat until he choked.

Papa pointed out the obvious. "It's in the town of Harper. This is the Harper Improvement Society."

"But it's for the colored," Mr. Minkie said. "Let them build their own school."

Mr. Yampell started to talk, but Papa put his hand up, saying, "I have here a paper signed by over two hundred members of the colored community who have requested a new school."

Someone whispered, "They can write?"

Papa kept right on going. "With the old Quince Road school as a high school and the Jefferson school for the young ones, they'd have plenty enough room."

"Coloreds in our school!" Mr. Cassell stood, knocking his chair back.

"Mr. Cassell, please." Mr. Yampell looked embarrassed. Mayor Kinley sat behind him smiling away like he watched a picture show. "We haven't determined a use for that building yet. We could put it to the town for a vote."

"There are nearly four hundred coloreds in this town, Mr. Yampell. You got two hundred folks voting on your Yankee ticket?" asked Clem Thibodeaux.

"Excuse me?"

I could feel the anger rising in the room like fog.

Papa stood up. "If they put the Quince Road school on logs and rolled it on down toward the swamp, would that make you feel better?"

My heart shrunk. Papa wanted to keep the black folks living in the worst part of town?

"It'd be a start." Clem Thibodeaux crossed his arms in front of him. His brother, Merle, shook his head as if disgusted.

Papa leaned over toward him. "It'd be the same building, Clem. With the same children in it."

I smiled, hiding my face behind the book I pretended to read.

"Don't you mock me, Bergen." Clem wagged a finger at Papa.

"I'm not, Clem. I figured you simply needed a little clarification of things, seeing as how this is your first time meeting with us." He turned to the whole group. "Mr. Yampell had the right idea. We put it to a vote. Sheriff Talson has agreed to oversee the voting since he's still in town on the arson investigation. Then I think we should interview teachers for both schools, Mrs. Owens." He nodded toward Mrs. Owens, who sat at the end of the table, keeping her weak eyes focused on her hands. Everyone knew the Northerners wanted her fired, but she'd been teaching at my school for a rock's age. "We'll conduct the interviews along with Mayor Kinley and Mr. Yampell."

The old Harper folks looked over at Mayor Kinley as if he were their last hope, and they regretted allowing Papa to get this far into things.

"And what about that arson investigation?" Mr. Minkie asked, forcing the conversation in a new direction.

Papa sat down, then nodded toward Sheriff Denton. "Sheriff."

"We are pursuing leads, but we have no suspects at this time."

"In other words you're chasing your own tails in the wind." Mr. Cassell cleared his throat. The other Harper men laughed. But not Papa or the Northerners. They cast their eyes on the table.

The sheriff rapped the table. "We have time. With a fire like this, there's no statute of limitations on murder."

"Who died in the fire?" Mr. Thibodeaux asked.

Mr. Minkie wanted to know: "Did Miss Chessie succumb to her injuries?

"Oh, did I say murder?" Sheriff Denton smiled. "I meant attempted murder."

The ruby-ring trio shifted in their seats but kept silent.

Mr. Yampell moved on to talk about bringing refrigeration into the mercantile, but I didn't pay him any mind. Hunting for a suitable school for the black folks I'd turned my thinking to the buildings in town that didn't have any clear use. In a flash an idea sprouted up inside me like a magic beanstalk. Dropping my book, I charged up the steps, then wound my way right up to Mama's studio. She hadn't built a door to knock on, so I went right in.

"Mama!"

Swirling on the tall chair she had in front of a canvas, she said, "Yes, ma'am."

"How about a Belmin Family Memorial?"

"Say again?"

"We fix up the church his brother built. Remind folks of what he tried to do. What they died for."

"That's a fine idea, Nissa." Mama smiled.

"And howdy." I hadn't felt so blood rushing good since I'd thought of building a library. "We'll have to get a town vote."

Mama gave me her look-at-that-girl-go stare. "Uh-huh."

"I'm going down to suggest it right now."

Mama laughed. "You do that."

I was already on the stairs before she finished talking. Charging into the room as folks started to collect their things, I shouted, "I've got something."

"What's that?" Papa asked, but the other folks stared at me as if I'd asked them to swallow fire.

"Well, you know how we're preserving our town's first school?"

Clem Thibodeaux glared at Papa. "We're trying to."

"I think we should also have a memorial to Horace Belmin and his family in the church Davis Belmin built."

"The Belmins?" Mr. Yampell asked. The other Northerners looked just as curious. Clem Thibodeaux, Mr. Cassell, and Mr. Minkie went pale, looking like I'd staked them in the heart.

Turning my back on them, I told the Northerners about Pastor Belmin. Leaving the killers to stew in their own guilt, I kept their names a secret. But I made the point real clear that a memorial to the Belmins might keep folks from doing anything like that—or setting fire to a cannery—ever again. Most of the folks at the table nodded in agreement with the idea.

As I finished, Pastor Linzy cleared his throat to say, "Pastor Belmin has long been regarded among his peers as a visionary. A prophet, if you will. Our church will gladly honor his memory with a donation."

Mrs. Linzy went stiff, but her husband didn't pay her any mind.

"I think it'd be a fine idea." Mr. Yampell smiled

The mayor shifted in his seat, saying, "We don't have the public funds for it."

"I'll donate money. My wife can start a fund drive," Mr. Yampell offered.

The sheriff put his hand up like he'd started to direct traffic. "I don't know if it's the right time to do this. People are still quite upset."

"That makes it just the right time to do it." Mrs. Owens looked straight at him. "We need to remind people of what hatred like that can do."

Mr. Cassell flushed red, but he didn't speak. Was he mad? Ashamed? He should've been on his knees begging God's forgiveness.

Clem Thibodeaux certainly wasn't. He mumbled to himself,

his hands over his chest, while Merle nodded his head to agree with Mrs. Owens. The Minkies held hands. I'd never seen them do that before.

Mr. Yampell said, "Unless anyone challenges it, I say we build this Belmin Family Memorial Nissa suggested. My wife will be the chief fund-raiser." I couldn't get over how this fella just gave his wife a job without even asking her first. The way everyone else just took it as natural told me I'd stumbled over another Heirah-and-Ivar custom I'd learned—women make their own decisions. I had no plans to change my thinking on this one.

Mr. Yampell smiled, saying, "Anything else?"

No one spoke. I figured I'd made enough ground for one evening, so I stayed quiet too.

"Then let's go on home."

Folks walked out chatting amongst themselves. Mr. Yampell congratulated me on a good idea. After a while, just Papa and I stood at the table. He smiled at me.

"So a memorial to the Belmins yanked you out of your seat and chased you upstairs to talk with your mama."

"That's right."

Papa came around the table and took my elbow. "Nissa, you best take better care now. You make me fill up with too much pride, and my little Norwegian heart's going to burst."

"Thanks, Papa."

We headed toward the stairs. Papa shouted up, "Heir-ah!" My, how I loved hearing him do that.

Mama came tromping down the stairs. "Coming, Ivar."

"Let's go tell Lara what we've gotten her into this time."

"Won't she be thrilled." Mama smiled, taking my other elbow. We headed on out the door, arm in arm, like a regular old family.

Building

uilding new things seemed like the right response to a fire set by hatred. One crew worked on the cannery, which had already returned to business as usual. The WPA folks hurried to keep Mr. Yampell's promise of a new school by October. In time Ira and Mama got the chance to head up the church crew. In a vote held in the veterans' hall, the scene of Mama's mayoral debacle, the town voted on the memorial and the old Quince Road school.

Clem Thibodeaux actually raised Papa's idea—why not move the school? He said "our" children (like he had any!) deserved to have a strong education without the undue influence of others. I suppose he didn't want any news of folks like Marcus Garvey or W. E. B. Du Bois to drift over from the colored school. I found out from books in the library that those two fellas had the advancement of colored folks utmost on their minds. So did the colored folks voting that night in the veterans' hall.

For them, getting in required a lot more than the two feet it took for the white folks in town to be allowed to enter the hall.

The sheriffs stood outside sending the colored folks to a table under the window, saying they had to register to vote.

Mrs. Villeneuve pointed at the Minkies as they went inside. "Have they registered?"

Sheriff Denton lied, saying, "They're registering inside. We don't have enough room in there to register everyone."

"Registration," as he called it, consisted of signing in, if you were white. The black folks had to stand in line outside. Once they got up to Mr. Cassell, they had to answer all sorts of questions. Do you own property in Harper? Have you voted in parish or state elections for the past five years? Can you read and write? If they answered no to any one question, they were sent home.

I knew for a fact half the white folks inside couldn't answer yes to all of those questions. Heck, every Yankee in town couldn't say they'd even voted in the last state election. As crooked as a live oak tree, the registration process only allowed about fifty black folks inside.

When the "town" tried to send the old school down into the swamp, Mrs. Villeneuve and Miss Carver, who taught at the colored school on Jefferson, stepped up to the side windows. Miss Carver said, "Our building has dry rot from all the water down there. We can't keep the place dry when it rains. Why not move both schools to higher ground?"

Mr. Villeneuve, Ira, Rinnie Lee, Mr. Garver, and Mr. Beaurigard all joined those ladies. Ira said, "We've all"—he motioned to those around him—"collected money and purchased the land between the Gator and the cannery. Mr. Yampell was kind enough to give us a good price." Eyes turned on Yampell. "We'd like to have both schools moved up there."

Mama jumped up and shouted. "Put it to a vote!"

Lara followed suit. So did Papa, the Rosses, and even

Grandpa Knute, who'd never seen Harper before, but no one asked him to register. If I could've voted, I would've joined them. But we had ourselves a family coalition all right.

And it pushed folks to vote. By a margin of two, the Jefferson Street school, soon to become the West Harper School, was set to move just west of the West Harper Library. My west-to-east divide had really taken hold. This time for the better. True enough, those folks deserved a new school like ours, but they'd been given room to grow.

Then came the vote on the memorial. I stood in front of all those people, knowing my words would be enough to set me in their minds as a troublemaker. "Pastor Horace Belmin came to this parish with his mind set on the ideas of Jesus. Wear simple clothes. Put your heart into worship. Treat your fellow children of God as equals regardless of where they came from, what they look like, or what folks say about them. And for his beliefs the pastor and his family were burned to death in the church where he spoke the Word of God."

As I talked, some of the black folks in the audience punctuated my sentences with "amen"s and kept me going. "I grew up in this town, and I never heard of Pastor Belmin until last year. Hiding the crimes of the past only raises the chance that such crimes will be committed again. The terrible fire at the cannery will bear that truth out. So I propose that our town repair the old church on Charleston Road in honor of Pastor Belmin and build a memorial to his whole family there."

Mr. Cassell nearly growled as he said, "Thank you, Miss Bergen."

I'd heard more noise in a graveyard than in that room. Then, quiet like, Papa said, "Shall we have a vote?"

Mama answered, "Yes."

Papa started it off. "In favor?"

The "aye"s came in slow. First Mr. Beaurigard, then the Yampells, the Villeneuves, and in a surprise turn, the Minkies—and as more hands went up, folks felt more confident and started voting. The motion carried with 567 votes, and that was with nearly 300 people barred from the building.

Mrs. Yampell started collecting money, and even with some families only able to give food for the volunteers, he had enough for repairs faster than it takes to cure salt pork. Mr. Thurston tipped the scales when he agreed to donate lumber, brushes, and buckets. Ira hired a crew. They started with the rotting floor and worked their way up. As the church came back to its old glory one board at a time, I asked Mama to show me how to chisel so I could make a plaque for the Belmin Family Memorial. While she stained the church's windows with paint, I chiseled away.

I worked in Mama's studio for a time. Every now and again I heard the hum of the cannery. They still hadn't tracked the fire starters down. I wondered if they ever would. Folks went to work like nothing ever happened. The cannery didn't show a single scar. A jagged patch of bare ground stood as the only reminder of what had happened there that summer. I prayed grass would never grow over it.

Seeing that bare, raw earth, I thought of Miss Chessie holed up in her brother's house. I knew she didn't want to be seen, but I had to at least pay my—no, I couldn't say I respected her, but I sure did feel the need to say how sorry I was that such an awful thing happened to her.

I picked her a bouquet of flowers from our garden, then I headed on over. Standing on the porch, I realized I stood at the door of Peter Roubidoux, a boy who participated in a beating that could've taken my life. I near about turned around, but I knocked instead. Mrs. Kate Roubidoux answered the door.

"Afternoon, Nissa."

"These are for Miss Chessie." I showed her the flowers.

"How are you feeling?"

"Fine." I nodded.

"Good. Good."

"Is Miss Chessie seeing visitors?"

"I'll check." She opened the door wider. "Come on in and have a seat."

Miss Kate headed off down the hall. I sat down in the parlor. I heard footsteps and expected Miss Kate, but Peter came in instead. I stiffened.

"Nissa." He didn't even look me in the eye. "I never meant for no one to get hurt."

"What did you mean then, Peter?"

"I . . ." His voice rose like he wanted to yell, then fell. "I was a fool. Going off like that leads to awful things." He shook his head and even sounded like he might cry.

"I'm sorry about your aunt Chessie."

"I didn't do it!"

"I never said you did." Though having him shout like that made me wonder.

"I don't even know who did." He turned toward the wall. "That sheriff comes here every day, asking me things, expecting me to break down and confess. I've got nothing to confess." He looked up, his face lily pale, his eyes ringed in black. No, he had nothing to confess except how guilty he felt about the whole thing.

"I understand, Peter."

"You believe me, don't you, Nissa?"

"I do."

Miss Kate appeared in the hallway. "Chessie will see you, Nissa."

I followed Miss Kate to a shadowy bedroom in the back of the house. Miss Chessie sat by the window, a scarf on her head, her face turned away from me.

"I brought you flowers."

"Put them there." Without moving her head, she pointed to a bureau by the closet. Vases lined the thing. Right in the center stood a blue vase filled with purple roses so deep you'd think they'd been petaled in the velvet of a queen's cape—my mama's roses. She'd been there too.

I put my flowers in a vase, then took a seat in the corner across from Miss Chessie. I said, "Times like these, there's no real good thing to say, is there?"

Miss Chessie cast her good eye at me. "I figured you and your mama would be glad to see me like this."

"Not at all."

She licked her lips, and I could see how raw and sore they looked at the edges. I felt the pain of it in my own mouth. "I know. Your mama came. She brought me roses. Her roses. And a darn tree." Chessie looked at me, the right side of her face looking as raw and scarred as a tree that'd been attacked by termites and stripped of its bark. I had all I could do to keep from shrinking back. "So I could plant it and start life anew. Your mama said that to me." Chessie cried.

I couldn't talk. Not only because I didn't have the words, but on account of the fact that I had no right to speak just then. I had to give her room.

"Your mama knows all about starting over, I see that now. Damn her for being the better woman. She makes it awful hard to sit here and feel sorry for myself." She laughed. "Now you, coming here. . . . You didn't bring me a tree, did you?"

I laughed. "No, only flowers."

"Good." She stared out the window. "I gave your mama money for the church. A place like that needs to be kept up."

"Yes, ma'am."

Chessie closed her eyes. When she opened them again, she looked right at me. "Your mama raised you up right after all."

And with that, I cried too.

Trials, Traveling Schoolhouses, and Changes Yet to Come

The sirens sent everyone to their windows wondering if another fire had been started. The sheriffs drove into town with two men in the backseat, boys really—probably not much older than Peter and Teddy. I'd seen them around the factory, but I didn't even know them by name.

Lara brought the story back from the post office that evening. Mississippi boys, they claimed someone paid them two hundred dollars each to set the fire. But neither one could say who hired them. They'd been contacted by phone at the hotel and paid in cash in an envelope slid under their door. Had Mr. Cassell done it? He ran the darn hotel. Heck, the town switchboard sat just off his lobby. There'd be no way to know. Those boys got shipped to the parish courthouse to stand trial.

Their arrest made me wonder after Simon again. Papa didn't want me visiting the boy. I knew Simon had meant to do me serious harm, but it still didn't seem right to break his leg. Dr. Swenson said he shouldn't stand trial until he mended. I figured Dr.

Swenson was doing another family service like he used to do for Papa. The Carrolls wanted time with their boy, and he saw to it that they got it.

Mary'd told me, Simon intended to plead guilty because he knew he'd done wrong and he aimed to get a lesser sentence for admitting to that fact. Mrs. Carroll called our place regular to see how I fared, but since that morning of prayer, I hadn't seen her. Mama said to give her time to grieve. Her child hadn't died, but Mama was sure it felt that way to her.

To keep my mind on better things to come, I went to the library the day after the arrest to work on my plaque for the memorial. Sitting in the West Library, I could see the work crew edging my old schoolhouse across the field. They'd moved it over Sutton's Creek on logs they dropped into the water, then rolled it right onto a train bed. The train brought it to the back of the Gator, then they had to hoist it down the bank on a row of logs thick enough to hide a family inside. It was a spectacle to admire. The old Jefferson Street schoolhouse turned out to be too rotten to move, so they had to collect money to build new. They raised less money for that than Mrs. Yampell did for the memorial, but the state and the New Dealers chipped in too. Turned out those folk did end up with the new school they deserved after all. Well, with a new school anyway, maybe not the one they deserved.

By the time Mama had the church windows painted I had my plaque ready. It told the story of Pastor Belmin and his family. Ira hung it on the front door of the church.

That Sunday a whole group of us gathered together to dedicate the memorial. The Crocked Gator crowd came, even Leo, who had ugly scars to show for his pain. Ira's whole crew showed up. So did the Northerners who had no roots in Harper soil, but in my way of thinking, they knew how to start the sowing right.

Mrs. Owens came. As did Mr. Beaurigard, Dr. Swenson, Mr. Hess, Eloise Simpson, and her sister. The Carrolls all came, even Simon, with Sheriff Denton at his side. The Roubidouxs showed up, escorting Miss Chessie in a fine new hat and a Sunday dress. She looked pretty and frail.

After reading the plaque out loud I opened the doors. Dust free and filled with the ambers, blue grays, and oranges of sunlight through painted glass, the place would've done Pastor Belmin proud. Most of the white folks, including my used-to-be best friend Mary Carroll, took to the left of church, but the West Harper folks and all of my kin did as God intended. We all sat down, black and white, hands locked together, and prayed—giving Pastor Belmin a small glimpse of what he'd always wanted to see.

Indeed, Harper was finally building up for a better future. I felt proud to be a part of it. God only knew what we'd create next.